THE JAGUAR ORACLE

A Mystical Animal Tale in a Series of Novellas

Book One
The Trail to the Lonely Tree

Written by

Kurt Frederick Mähler

Illustrated by

Monike Garabieta

To a fellow traveler in becoming a wordsmith.

9 April 16

ISBN: 1500551643
ISBN 13: 9781500551643

For Karen

Because of you, I remember the story I live in.

"Everything is linked with everything, and the clearly visible relations of things have their roots in the night into which I am groping my way."

—A. G. Sertillanges
(1863–1948)

CONTENTS

CHAPTER 1

ORACLE OF SIAN KA'AN

I N the Yucatán of Mexico lived a jaguar named Oracle. His home was a realm of marshes and mangrove channels the Mayans had named *Sian Ka'an*: "Birthplace of the Sky." Thick stands of palm, cedar, and mahogany trees grew where a score of Mayan towns had once flourished, as their root-choked ruins and silent shipping canals testified. Creatures winged and four-footed dwelled there now with their neighbor, Man, who lived in fishing villages on the coast and who toured Sian Ka'an to enjoy its wonders, both beneath the shade of its bounty and on the clear, blue waters near its shores.

One morning in September, Oracle was keeping watch on his regular path through Sian Ka'an. Oracle crossed each canal with the seamless ease of one at home in the water. He was, of course, equally at home on land, though his body did not carry the genteel gait of an African cat, nor of an Asian one. Oracle, like all jaguars, walked with a kind of plodding gentleness, reminiscent of a servant treading grapes in the press of a vineyard or a farmer bringing home the heavy gleanings of the day.

The low beams of the rising sun made their way through the leaves and branches and splashed upon the jaguar's rosette-spotted coat: fluid circles set on a field of ruddy gold. The ground was cool beneath Oracle's feet. The night air was still in the soil, though the day had already warmed to the low-grade fever of summer. Wading in a shallow pond, a jabiru bird watched the cat pass by. In the tall grass, an agouti foraged, solemn of face yet gentle of form, not unlike a guinea pig. In the branches above, a goldfinch sang his joyful song. A macaw spread his plumage, emerald green and indigo blue, in squawking response to the cheer of the goldfinch. A wide-winged frigate bird swept by and disappeared, banking through the airy pathways among the trees. Oracle slowed, halted, and sampled the air. He growled softly.

"All is well with what I see, but all is not well with what I sense," he said.

The jabiru cocked his head to listen.

"A Man approaches," the macaw announced from above. "A Man with a coat—a jaguar coat."

"He is a shaman of the mantribes," Oracle said, "a knower of the tongues of the bodiless ones and where they dwell."

"He has been here since the gray of dawn," the agouti muttered, lowering his head beneath the grass. "He walks back and forth, playing a wooden bow whose strings have a voice." The agouti backed into the foliage as if to put distance between himself and the secret he had just revealed.

"What does he seek?" Oracle asked.

"He seeks no kill, to be sure," called the macaw. "I see no weapon save the one for rituals in the caves. And his bow—how strange!— many strings, but no arrow! He is not here to hunt."

"And yet he is hunting," Oracle said, "for he comes at the time of surprise."

A human footstep sounded. A faint ring of small bells followed. The goldfinch silenced his song, the jabiru crouched with eyes staring, and the agouti bent to the angle of the grass to hide himself. But Oracle did not move; he remained in the center of the trail, looking toward the bend ahead of him as another footstep pushed upon the ground.

A Man appeared. He wore a ceremonial costume of leather and animal skin. On it were the spots of the jaguar. The headdress was the face of the animal, with the shaman's own face—painted black and yellow—disclosed between the jaws. Eagle feathers topped the headdress. Dismembered paws covered the tops of the Man's feet, upon which he wore embroidered sandals with leather straps that wrapped up his legs to the knees. Bells and tassels hung from his elbows. A tail dangled behind.

In the shaman's hands was the wooden bow that the agouti and the macaw had described. It looked like a small harp or lyre; the curved Brazilian rosewood held sinews of a jungle cat. Attached to one side of the harp was a cowl of skin for deepening the sound. The shaman strummed. The jabiru sprang free of the water and flew away.

Oracle heard the voice of a jaguar, but it was odd—dead, yet alive. It was familiar but clumsy. It sounded as if someone—a relative? an impostor?—was giving the jaguar's call, but the sound did not belong to Oracle's tribe. He was sure of that, because the roar lacked the part of his call that was deeper than the call itself: the cry behind the call.

Then, from the midst of the thick leaves of the marshes, where shadow still prevailed over the morning light, a spirit blew past Oracle. An arctic shudder followed it, a blast from a door that swung shut as quickly as it had opened. The spirit panted in thirst.

"Where is a house I can dwell in?" it rasped, distressed by the soulless air.

The strange, strumming call of the shaman's lyre continued. Oracle listened carefully.

"What is this," he thought, "that the sound of the manharp, so close to my own voice, conjures spirits to come running to it? I have heard the shaman call on spirits before, but never have I heard a voice like this! Only tales from the deep past on fractured walls and broken pots hint of such things in the heart of the jungle."

The spirit hovered in a pocket of air above the grass and beneath the trees. It darted back and forth like a betta fish trapped in too small a bowl. Its eyeless face shot a glance toward the agouti, who, already cowering, sensed the desperation of the searching spirit. The agouti dove for the nearest bush and ran. The spirit turned its craving gaze toward the macaw in the branches above. The bird threw his wings open full length, screaming threats. But the spirit glowered, unafraid, and the parrot rose, flapping frantically, angry that the air would not thrust him away faster.

The spirit turned and faced Oracle, who looked at it with his fangs bared and claws flared. Hunger grew in the bodiless, cold thing as it looked upon the warm body of the jungle cat.

"Let me in," it whispered.

"I will not," Oracle replied.

"You are my house!" said the spirit, raising its voice. "I am called by your name. I dwell where jaguars dwell."

"You dwell where fear dwells," Oracle replied, "and there is no fear in my house."

The spirit murmured a sound between a growl and a rattle. "Your kind obeys me," it said.

"*Your* kind obeys you. I am not of your kind."

"Our stories go together," said the spirit. "They always have. Let me in that you might live in my story."

"My story is older than your story and more beautiful," Oracle replied. "That is the story I live in. I will not live in your story, for I am no dwelling place for a lesser tale. My tale comes from the time before the animals forgot their names."

"Ah! I know who you are, oh cat! You are of the Ones Who Remember! You hold on to the myths! Lies, they are. All lies. Look before you. This is what is real. Forget the old stories and live in mine."

"No," growled Oracle, and he fought the urge to flee.

"Disobedience will bring disaster," the spirit threatened.

"The disaster is to conform to your threats."

"Let me in, or I will curse you."

"To let you in *is* the curse. To keep you out is the blessing."

"You are my place!"

"Only if I give it to you. You have no place in me otherwise. Go."

"If I go, you will die. You only live because I give you power."

"I only live because I know who I am. Now *go*."

"Curse you!" the spirit cried out. "Curse you and all your line! False jaguar, I say! False to your tribe! False to your flesh! False to me, to me—I who have the power to save or to destroy!"

"Your words boast power, but powerless they are to make me forget my name. I remember Eden. I remember what Adam said. This is my power. This keeps me alive. It is greater than your fear. It is greater than your spell."

The spirit gathered itself into a concentrated form with clawed paws and unsheathed fangs. It shivered with hate until, like a spout venting steam, out came a gasping, shrieking call.

"Disobedience!" the spirit cried. "Disobedience! I prophesy your doom! I pronounce your fall! I curse you with disaster! Disaster! Disaster!" The spirit chanted:

Down with you and death with you;
May each and every fear come true!
A curse on all you taste and touch!
A curse on all you love so much!
A loss of all you hope to gain!
A turn of pleasure into pain!
A weary drought instead of rain!
Dust be your food, and drink in vain!

The spirit swirled into a tornado of rage, blew through the tops of the trees, and disappeared, searching for a dwelling that would take it in while its howling faded away.

The shaman, meanwhile, marveled at his harp. He turned his eyes toward Oracle, who still remained in the center of the trail. The shaman, shaking and cold, approached him reverently. He touched the jaguar on the head and looked about him in fretful wonder. Then, in an ancient tongue that only the hieroglyphs of the crumbling ruins could understand, he asked the beast for forgiveness. He spoke words of blessing, bowed, and departed. Oracle watched him go.

The jaguar from the tribe of the Ones Who Remember looked at the place in the branchy jungle roof through which the spirit had fled. Oracle found that he was more fatigued than he had expected, as if he had just finished a long climb uphill. In silence he allowed solitude to fill the empty space above him until it became full of peace. Then Oracle licked his paws (like all cats great and small do) and waited in the stillness. If you had seen him just then, you would not have known that a moment before he had been at war. Then he continued on his path through Sian Ka'an.

* * *

That afternoon, in the heat of the day while he rested, Oracle dreamed. In his dream he was walking though the wetlands of Sian Ka'an. He came upon a lion, serene and terrible to behold. And yet, the innocence of the lion was so disarming that Oracle remained transfixed in gazing upon him. And he saw that the lion was more beautiful than terrible. Beside the lion flowed a river—chattering, cheerful, and crystal clear—whose riverbed was covered with every kind of precious stone Oracle knew and others he had never seen before. The sunlight burst back off the stones in every color of the rainbow and more.

"It is the Lion of Eden," Oracle thought to himself, though no one in the dream had told him so. He went close and bowed.

The lion rose and licked the top of Oracle's head. Then the lion reclined sphinxlike before the jaguar in a pose reminiscent to Oracle of the way the leaders of the jaguar tribes reclined when they held court. Behind the lion stood a tall banana tree.

The lion spoke to Oracle. He employed a dialect of the feline tongue unique to the jaguars of the Yucatán, a dialect spoken only at rites of passage or counsels of war or funerals.

"What will you give for this banana tree?"

Oracle considered the tree. Many of the bananas were overripe, some even black and dangling by a half stem, though a few were green. Oracle held out his paw and turned it up toward the lion.

"One paw," said Oracle, "for the sake of the green. The black and the yellow belong to the air and to the sun."

"What if the sun will not have the yellow?" asked the lion.

"For them I give two," replied Oracle. "If the heat comes, I will cover them."

"What if the air will not have the black?"

"For them I give three. If they drop, I will gather them."

"And the root?" the lion asked.

Oracle looked at all four of his feet. "Here is my all—heart, head, and paws."

"How is it that you give more for the root than the fruit?" the lion asked.

"The root is the life of the stalk and all she bears—yellow, black, and green," he replied. "Life is worthy of life, and therefore she may have mine."

The lion began to sway as if in temple chant. His mouth was closed, but a song began to fill Oracle:

This is the way: my right I lay
Down at the root, kaloo, kalay
This is my hope by night or day
Rivers of joy, kaloo, kalay
Hold out your paw to me, I say
Give me your all, kaloo, kalay
Fear not the pall that draws today
Honey from gall, kaloo, kalay.

The river rose as the lion sang—its chatter also singing, its waters flooding, plunging the jungle and the banana tree and the lion and the jaguar beneath its waves. Yet nothing was swept away or drowned. Instead, all became washed and clear, and Oracle found he could breathe more deeply beneath the river than before when he had been on dry ground. And for the first time, Oracle noticed that the lion was no longer there, though he could not recall the exact moment when he had disappeared. In the lion's place was a host of animals, some of whom were familiar to the jaguar, but many Oracle had never seen before—animals ruddy and dusty, animals bejeweled and beautiful, animals lonely and proud, animals calling the call of their kinds. Then Oracle realized the banana tree was gone, and in its place a long, sandy seashore stretched down and away from him to the horizon before a sunset surf.

Oracle awoke. It was dusk. Through the jungle canopy above, he saw the glint of the three-quarter moon as the departing sun loaned his glory to her. Oracle arose, shook off the sleep of his body, and gazed up at the shining moon.

"I will not be here much longer," he said.

He touched the jaguar on the head and looked about him in fretful wonder.

CHAPTER 2

THE SIGH OF THE BUTTERFLY

—————

THE morning light flooded an October sky washed clean. Rainwater still dripped from leaves and flowers. All night long it had poured as if the sky's supply had been without limit. But in the quiet of the dark before the dawn, the exhausted storm made her silent departure. The sun found no cloud to greet him when he rose.

Oracle came out from under broad leaves bent heavy with water. He breathed the fresh air. All was still. The animal kingdom was in no hurry to disturb the great calm. It was a gift they savored.

But a faint sound came to Oracle that was not calm. It was a sigh, a whisper from someone too tired to speak. Oracle turned his ears. He walked toward the sound. The rain-drenched grass and fresh pools bathed him as he moved, but Oracle kept his gaze toward the direction of the sighing. Then the foliage broke open before him to reveal the crumbled limestone of a forgotten Mayan temple—a shattered platform that had once been the foundation of a building grand and tall. Thick vines—some old and woody, some supple and green—grew over the stones, which, though motionless, seemed to be shattered by the vines that split through them. Oracle ascended a set of stairs half melted into grass.

Then he saw her. Atop the weatherworn surface of a fractured column, a monarch butterfly lay on her side, laboring to breathe.

Her wings rose and fell according to the straining body beneath them, but in them was no flight. One was broken.

Oracle placed his muzzle beside her and drew in the scent of the waters of the Gulf of Mexico and a faraway land of humid air, of trees, and of the hardened paths of Man that pass through them.

"Hail, Windblown One," he said. "How did you get here?"

The monarch could only look at him. Oracle saw that Death was looking at her, considering when to stiffen her form after one last breath.

"She cannot die," Oracle thought with a sense of ardor, "for she still has a story within her she must tell."

Turning, he leaped to the highest point of the ruin, a fallen, flat slab. He surveyed the undergrowth about him until his eyes found the bright hints of flowers. He bounded there, splashing the sleeping raindrops of the jungle as he jumped through it. Oracle found a hibiscus bush, whose fuchsia blooms gently cradled the offspring of the night's fierce storm, droplets pearl-like in shape and in shine.

Oracle chose the one whose fragrant sweetness reached into him most deeply. He grasped its stem with his jaws, plucked it off, and bounded back toward the monarch.

"Here, sister," Oracle said. "Take and drink. The same storm that blew you here will provide your healing."

And the butterfly drank a drop of rain.

The strength of the night's windy sky moved through her, and the monarch found grace to probe the heart of the hibiscus. She found nectar and drank deeply. Every swallow revived her, and though it did not restore her wing, it restored her song.

"Hail," she spoke softly. "Hail, lord of this unknown place. Hail to you and thank you."

You found me frail
A dry leaf doomed
To dust below
In earthen tomb

You brought the drop
On nectar vase
I drank the storm
And drank in grace.

"You are welcome," Oracle replied. "This place may be unknown to you, but it is known to me. This is Sian Ka'an, of the manrealm known as the Yucatán."

"How far am I from the Singing Mountain?" the monarch asked. "For that is where I was traveling, along with one hundred thousand friends, to our forest home that rests in its shadow."

"The Singing Mountain?" asked Oracle. "I have heard of the place, but only in tales. It is far from here in the heart of the high cliffs of the manrealm known as the Michoacán."

"Yes, but the stones here sing like those of the Michoacán," the monarch replied. "They sing the song of the Singing Mountain. These broken pieces of the forgotten manplace have in them the ore that makes the song. I hear it. It sustained me while I lay here until you came."

"Then these ruins no doubt are of stones from your home," he said. "Man brought them here for reasons that belong to him. Whether mindful of you or not, I do not know, but the stones themselves continue to be the singing stones they were at the mountain. They have not forgotten their song."

"Yes, and I am thankful, for their song reached me in the night sky of the storm. They told me there was solid ground below. The song rescued me, and your gift restored me."

"You were on your way to the Singing Mountain?"

"Yes, it is the odyssey of my kind in the House of Lepidoptera each year. We gather on the branches of the forest in the shadow of the mountain, and we tell one another the tales we have heard from the flowers we have visited across the Great Continent of the North. We gather and tell tales and begin our own tale again. This is why we call our home the Forest of Tales. But a great thunderstorm with wind and crashing spears swept down upon us and drove us above the gulf waters. We flew high but could not overcome it. We flew east but could not go around it. We flew down, but lo, there was nothing to rest upon, not even the tall steel towers of Man, who draws with them the black gold from beneath the sea. So we labored and bid farewell to one another—some to the shroud of the clouds, others to the blasts of the battling winds, and others to the sea below, who received them when the strength of the nectar of a thousand flowers had been spent.

"But I, in the black wild of last night, heard the song from these stones, just as the cold fire of the storm broke out with such force that my wing snapped. I fluttered and spun but took courage and let my body drop. And behold, I am here. And you are here. Thank you."

The sun climbed, and the rock where she rested grew quite warm. Oracle asked the monarch for permission to move her, and she obliged. Now, a jaguar's whiskers are very sensitive things, such that even in utter darkness, they serve as a set of feeling eyes to tell the cat the precise shape of what is close at hand. And so it was that with this skill, Oracle felt the damaged portion of the monarch's wing, which, though attached, was bent. With the moisture of his tongue, Oracle raised the butterfly just near enough to his lips so as to hold but not harm the wounded monarch. He carried her to the shade of a hibiscus bush nearby and laid her on a broken temple stone. The stone's ore, though lost from home for a millennium, still knew the song of the Singing Mountain it had come from and sang to her.

That night, the jaguar lay down beside the monarch.

"I will keep watch while you are healing," he said. "Tomorrow I will place you among the hibiscus flowers above. They will give you sweet shelter for whatever length of days remains to you."

"Thank you for keeping watch," the monarch said, "but it is night—your time to find food."

"My food this night will be the stories you tell me," Oracle replied. "The storm has blown you far away from your friends and your home; you will have to make do with a cat and a stone. Let this be your storytelling place. I am no butterfly, but I have ears to hear. Tell me your story."

The monarch took heart. She raised herself on six thin legs and bowed.

"A wise saying and a good one," she said, and she mused in silence before continuing.

"Perhaps the storm was not as wild as I had thought, but it tamed my intent to go where I had wanted to go. Anything less than a storm would not have deterred me from finding the Singing Mountain. We are monarchs; we are determined to find the Forest of Tales. A storm was the gentlest way to change my direction. And lo, as I contemplate, the wildness seems even less wild but rather *willed*. The tale I have is one that will make your eyes bright and your ears open, for it is a tale of a *jaguar*. The fragrant, white blossoms of the anacua tree told it to me as I browsed among them in the manrealm known as the Rio Grande Valley."

And she sighed as she considered the story that paced back and forth before her mind's eye.

Oracle sighed as well, composed but attentive. And while the moon climbed above them, he took in the words of his broken-winged guest as she told the Tale of the Last Jaguar.

* * *

"I dwelled among the blooms of South Texas in the realm of the Great River of the North, what Man also calls the Rio Grande. There I heard the flowers whisper of things from long ago. They spoke odes to the end of one tree age and the beginning of another— odes that, when I heard them, made my wings become slow with sorrow: mesquite trees supplanting olives and tallows supplanting ash. The citrus pushing out the cypress and the hackberry the sabal palm. Cedar posts standing where cedar trunks once grew, and long, straight ironthorn replacing the long, crooked branches of the ebony. The flowers sang of Man subduing the wilderness, first with spurred boots and leather armor to push aside the thorns, then with toothy iron machines to consume the thorns altogether.

"I learned that jaguars like you had ruled the animal kingdom in South Texas for many an age of Man—the age of the Karankawa and the Coahuiltecan, the age of the conquistador and the *explorateur* with flags bearing lions and castles and fleurs-de-lis. But in the age when Man raised the Lone Star against the flag with the eagle and the serpent, the well of life began to run dry for great cats like you. The flag of the eagle and the serpent fell, and the river delta was carved up and cordoned off. Day after day and night after night, the jaguars were hunted down. Sometimes Man fought wars with himself, and your kind found respite while he did. But he always returned to taming the land, and with each passing spring, there were fewer of your tribe to rule the animal kingdom.

"And so it was that the time came when only one jaguar remained: Kahoo the Grave. Yes, that is the name the flowers spoke. True to his name, he was solemn but good, they said. Every full moon he gathered the cats in counsel, the Cats of the Three Tribes: ocelot, bobcat, and mysterious jaguarundi. (The third cat I never saw, but I heard rumors from the pond reeds whose shape is not unlike his tail.) Kahoo guided the cats with just judgments and settled their disputes, often with only minutes to spare between the adjourning of his court and the arrival of those hunting for him. Kahoo, so the flowers sang, also enforced a just peace with the coyotes who roamed the land and with the mountain lions who came in lonely exile from their defeated realms. 'Thus far you may go and no farther,' he decreed, setting boundary lines for their hunting grounds. And the coyotes and the cougars abided by his law, lest the toothsome consequence of disobedience come upon them.

"But Man hunted Kahoo, for the cattle did not like him, nor did their owners, who depended on beef and hoof and hide for their livelihood. One morning, they discovered fresh tracks and released their hounds in pursuit of Kahoo. The chase lasted all day, and the bravest of the hounds fell to the fierce paw of the jaguar. Men made a great circle of watch posts and held vigil till evening. They lit torches and burned underbrush. They cut him off. They closed in. They pursued Kahoo until he climbed an anacua tree, thick with white blossoms. Men surrounded the tree with their machines and burning lights and rods of fire-spitting iron—a hunting party of deeply accented men from both sides of the border between the manrealms of the United States and Mexico.

"Knowing it was the end, Kahoo climbed to the uppermost branches; the anacua blossoms embraced him with their fragrance in farewell. Kahoo lifted his head to the heavens and roared. The flowers heard what he said, and they remembered. And when I came to dwell among them, it was their descendants who told me this tale. Here is what Kahoo the Grave prayed:

Oh moon, hear!
Oh stars, listen to me!
I depart the earth this night to join my fathers,
But you remain, and you keep watch.
Do not leave this river delta bare.
Do not leave it unled forever.
Watch in my place, and wait with open eyes
Until another comes to lead the kingdom
From the north and from the sky,
From here to river's end!

"And with that, Man killed the last jaguar. They strung his body on a rope before a big, black box on three legs, which flashed its fake lightning long enough to capture the sight on black and white and gray; men and boys with unclear expressions, awkward eyes, and unsure mouths gathered about the spotted beast.

"'We have shot the jaguar,' their faces said, 'but now we do not know what to do. Where do we go from here in a catless land? We do not know the way.'

"Seventy seasons of spring have come and gone since the last jaguar died. But the anacua tree remembers, and she retells the tale each year to her blossoming offspring. And they remember, too, and they whisper it to one another. And so the tale came to me as I dwelled among them and among the branches of their mother, whom the blossoms call the Lonely Tree."

Oracle thought deeply on the words of the tale until his eyes became sluices of water on the brim of pouring.

"For seventy springs no jaguar has ruled?"

"Yes, sire, for seventy springs."

"The Cats of the Three Tribes: do they meet in counsel without him?"

"I do not know."

"And the coyotes?"

"They roam and howl, for I heard them in the night. But I do not know if they abide by anyone. And the cougars have joined the ghosts of Man."

Oracle let the silence of the night have the center of the tale as he waited for words to come to him. The moon began her descent to the far side of the sky; she waxed strong in silver expectation of the morning sun. And as she did, Oracle heard words moving slowly in the air, words so faint that Oracle had to be more still than the air itself to hear them.

"Kahoo's prayer has spoken," he said, "and my four paws have heard it. They must go to the Lonely Tree and tell her that Kahoo has not been forgotten. Then the Lonely Tree will no longer be alone—until another comes to lead the kingdom 'from the north and from the sky'—whoever that may be."

CHAPTER 3

ORACLE PUTS HIS PAW FORWARD

THE dawn awakened gold in the monarch's wings. Sable veins bordered each illumined shape like the lead of stained-glass windows. A long shadow threw itself beyond the body of the butterfly, revealing strength the body did not speak of.

"Thank you, friend from the Forest of Tales," Oracle said. "You have redeemed the storm by telling the story to me. Now I will find you a suitable home among the flowers above."

Oracle lifted the monarch in his great but tender muzzle by the bend in her broken wing. He surveyed the bushes and found a hibiscus generously wreathed with thick leaves. The jaguar set her there and breathed the soft, warm air of his mouth upon her as he let her go.

"I have listened to your tale with my ears, but now I will listen to your tale with my feet. I will go to where you heard it. This day I put my paw forward."

"Yes, I see, to answer Kahoo's prayer," she said. "But I am puzzled; the last jaguar prayed for a successor 'from the north and from the sky.' But you come from the south and from the earth. How can you fulfill such a prophecy?"

"I do not know," answered Oracle. "But it is not up to me. I cannot contain the prophecy any more than I can contain the moon and the stars to whom Kahoo prayed. But I can contain my four paws, for they are mine. I will give them to Kahoo's prayer. Something more than I must complete the words Kahoo spoke, even as something more than you completed your journey to Sian Ka'an. And who knows, but perhaps even Kahoo himself did not know how such a prophecy could be fulfilled. But in that place Kahoo prayed, on the border between Life and Death, bathing in the fragrance of the anacua blossoms and the glaring lanterns of Man, perhaps he saw what we cannot see, and so he spoke it. The invisible that he saw may be more solid than the ground we walk on. We shall see."

The monarch bowed in farewell. Oracle bowed, too, and purred a blessing:

The blossoming hibiscus
The lily of the field
The crocus and narcissus
A house to you will yield

Like mankind's Mount Parnassus
A dwelling place for song
A home of many muses
A healing of all wrong.

And so Oracle began the journey that became known to later generations of jaguars as the Trail to the Lonely Tree.

* * *

The path was long. The moon kept watch through nine turns of her fullness, while the cat passed through wilderness and countryside, through river and waste, through stagnant heat and smoke-stained air—the outskirts of manplaces. Fall fell to winter. The cold gave way to spring, which fainted into summer. The land changed as Oracle moved northward. It became drier. More and more of it he found flattened under the seal of the steamroller. Ranches and farms gave way to rows of homes and stores with garish signs stacked one upon the other to match the floors of the buildings they belonged to. At night, neon and argon nobly glowed in glass globes to push back the darkness, extending the time that Man could work and play and hunt so that even traveling at night became perilous. But night was nevertheless when he mostly traveled, for that is the jaguar way. His path often began at evening and continued until the morning sun had broken the cool of the dawn.

In the heat of a July day, Oracle reclined beneath an ancient allthorn tree, whose green thorns drew more strength from the sun than did the plant's small, slender leaves. The base was thornless and scored with many scars—a diary of the trials the plant had endured as a shrubby shelter for quail while it reached the stature of a tree. Each wound had been swallowed up over the years with thick, wise wood. The bark was cool and solid to the cat, who leaned on the trunk beneath the thick covering of the thorns.

"Greetings, Tree of Many Sorrows," Oracle said.

"Greetings, Cat of the Yucatán," replied the tree. "Where are you going?"

"I travel to the Great River of the North, the one Man also calls the Rio Grande. It is a realm where no jaguar has placed his paw for seventy springs."

"And you go to take your place there?"

"Yes, so that the jaguar from long ago may not be forgotten, nor his place remain empty. I must go in answer to his last words."

"It has taken seventy springs for his last words to reach you."

"And one storm-tossed traveler to bring the message."

"I know the place you are going," the allthorn said. "The quail tell me about it, for they hide in my thorny arms on their way to and from that realm."

"What do they tell you?"

"They sing laments to the Lady River, who once lavished her alluvial gifts upon the land, giving her rich loam year after year in floody joy when she rose to cover the earth and to birth her offspring ponds."

"Why does she no longer offer her gifts?"

"Man tamed her to extract her bounty more efficiently," the allthorn replied, "but the taming left her barren. She no longer gives birth to watery places but runs in obedient submission to the line apportioned her between two nations. The quail tell me she holds up quite nobly in her widowhood, though she thirsts for rain in these days of the brass sky. No rain has fallen in that land for many suns. Perhaps Man has overtamed the river's realm. He has even tamed its very name, for, though it is a delta plain, he has given it the name 'river valley' instead. He calls it *El Valle*: the Valley."

"Such is Man's royal prerogative," the jaguar replied. "For he is the Namer. He names us, and he names the lands and the waters we live in."

"The name Valley is nevertheless true, if not accurate," commented the allthorn, "for it portends the shelter of lush fruit and the shadow of lonely exile. You will find both there."

"Thank you for showing that to me," Oracle said. "Like your thorns, your thoughts penetrate the surface; in the name Valley, the word echoes more than the sound it makes."

Oracle stretched his body beside the allthorn. And for the rest of the day, as the sun turned the shadows of the branches through their courses on the ground, the cat and the tree recalled the primordial tale of when the animals first received their names. Here is a small portion of that tale.

* * *

The four rivers flowed toward the four horizons of the compass. The liquid crystal that was the first water washed over beds of precious stones—diamond and onyx and the kaleidoscope of gems in between. The sun summoned iridescence from beneath the water; every color of the rainbow danced in the currents. Tigris, Euphrates, Pishon, and Gihon—the rivers sang their splashes through low arches in the surrounding wall that lay beyond sight from the center of the vast garden estate. The rivers rushed out to nurture untamed, unnamed realms.

Adam had seen these sleeping dominions. His Maker had traveled with him through them all: rolling dunes, grassy hills, icy peaks, placid lakes, boiling geysers, bloom-wrecked jungles, evergreen forests, majestic glaciers, and cavernous waterfalls. His Maker had shown him the depths of the earth, the storehouses of Man's future: pigment for paintings, marble for beauty, silver for honor, gold for glory. He had shown him the depths of the seas, the teeming bounty of nations yet to be, the mouths of sunken grottos no one would enter for a thousand generations.

Awestruck, Adam turned to his Maker and asked, "Father, is all this for me?"

It was Adam's first question.

"Yes," his Maker said. "This is how much I love you. It is all yours."

This was the opening exchange of their first conversation. The dialogue of the gift had begun.

The Maker placed him in the garden estate. As he explored Eden, Adam named the animals. As occasion presented itself, each animal bowed to its lord in reverent submission and waited for its name to be spoken—for only through Adam could it have a voice.

Adam spoke, and his voice sounded like his father's.

The words Adam spoke awakened within each animal a thing that could only come alive through the words it heard. And the words were not just sounds; they were stories. For Adam combined observation with insight, such was the grace in eyes as clear and a heart as clean as his. So when each animal came before him, a name and a story flowed from the Namer's mouth like a river.

When the bear went before Adam, Adam spoke a name understandable only to the bear. And the story of that name told the bear who he was, what he should do, and what were his unique skills and nature. And yet, it was not complicated or burdensome. The name evoked that which already existed in the bear—his "bearness"— but which could not be unlocked until the bear's Namer had spoken. Adam spoke, the lock turned, and the bear became a bear indeed.

Time passed.
A choice was made.
The choice was honored.
Darkness fell.

On Adam's last day in Eden, the flaming sword drove him and his beloved Eve out through the gateway of the garden until the Tree of Life he left behind faded into the realm of dreams. A cold wind blew over Adam, and a bleak wind blew over the animals—a long winter wind, a ghost that withered the very seed of their marrow. Now marred and lost, the animals retained the way of doing things, but not the *why*. Alienated from their master, Man, *thrive* became *survive*. *Live* became *exist*. *Birth* became *reproduction*. *Inspiration* became *instinct*. They forgot their names.

And Man forgot his.

But a few animals did not forget. They remembered the names Adam had given them. When the blast of blind fear came upon their kin, driving them to the wild lands beyond Eden, they did not flee, even when many a fair flower burst into a bouquet of thorns around them, and trees like the allbloom became known as the allthorn.

Instead, they gathered, one by one, on an isle in the middle of the Gihon River. Why? Because a lion stood there, solemn yet beautiful, with a joy that emanated from the light of his eyes and the sheen of his fur. No one knew exactly when the lion had swum there, or why, but there he was. And as the animals fled Eden, now and then one would turn and notice the lion. The sight made fear a vapor and desire strong, and the animal would go to him, joining the others.

What a unique flock it was, that flock of the lion! They beheld one another, and they remembered the occasion in the form of a song. Below are a few verses of it, which the oriole preserved in the days of the Great Flood. She sang it during the Great Waiting, the forty days our ancestors rested in the Tomb of Fallen Trees upon the dark waters with Man. And any animal who had a heart to listen to the Song of the Oriole remembered. Here is a portion of what she sang:

A songbird, a marsh crane, a fierce-beaked falcon
A turtle, a rabbit, a beaver, a hog
A wombat, a kanga, a bottlenose dolphin
A raccoon, a leopard, a pony, a frog
A jaguar drenched with the life of the river
An owl from her home in the heart of a log
A mantis in prayer giving praise to the Giver
An elephant, orca, and friendly bulldog

They came to the island, the island of Gihon
They swam through the river, the river of life
They gathered together, they came to the lion
Claw, tooth, and feather, they did not know strife.
The lion was waiting, the lion, the lion
The bright one, he called them, the sun in his hair,
He breathed on the gath'ring, the lion, the lion
He breathed, and they took in the Eden-filled air.

The lion breathed on the animals, and they forgot their dread. They remembered Eden, and they lived in the names Adam had given them. The ghost did not whither their marrow. They knew who they were.

"Let us pass on the breath of this hour as long as we have breath to give," the elephant said. "Let us pass it on to our progeny, and let us share it with whoever may listen. And let us remember these things, though the Garden becomes forgotten, though it disappears altogether, though the memory causes us to groan amid the thorns when we see how far removed we are from Eden's lush clover. For the breath of this memory may be a seed of the Garden to come."

The animals bowed to the elephant and touched their foreheads to one another in solemn promise. Then they departed. The dolphin swam to the sea, the rabbit sprung over the wall to the east, and the turtle began her slow odyssey to the south.

Time passed, ages of ice and steam, of flood and drought, ages of both Man and beast. But the descendants of the Flock of the Lion carried on the breath of that memory. They breathed the breath received at Gihon Isle—the breath of the lion—and they breathed it onto anyone who desired to listen to the tale of the Flock of the Lion. And the lines continued, the lines of remembrance, the names Adam had given them—their true names.

The descendants of the jaguar on whom the lion had breathed journeyed far to the west. Other jaguars, those who had not been on Gihon Isle, journeyed west too—some so full of forgetfulness that they became servants of a great, bodiless darkness that needed the flesh of the carnivore to minister its fears to Man. But the jaguar who had breathed Eden's air was as different from those jaguars as snow is from hail. That jaguar became the father of a unique tribe: the Ones Who Remember. They carried on the tradition of telling the tale of the Flock of the Lion; they knew what the elephant of Eden had called "the breath of this memory." They remembered Gihon Isle. They remembered their names.

Time passed. Forgetfulness fell on the jaguar's realm of rain and forest, of marsh and mountain. The face of the earth grew old. But the descendants of the Gihon Isle jaguar did not forget. They continued to breathe in Eden. They continued to remember. And, like all the other descendants of the Flock of the Lion, they passed on that breath to any who desired it, to any who would listen, and to any who would bend the head before the breath.

The jaguar set her there and breathed the soft, warm air of his mouth upon her.

CHAPTER 4

KISSING LADY RIVER

———

THE story ended. The allthorn contemplated the north, where Oracle faced still basking in the light of the tale.

"You are going to a land where the animals have forgotten their names, oh Cat Who Remembers," said the tree. "You are of the Flock of the Lion. You have not forgotten. I know. I see."

"How do you know?" Oracle asked. "For many can sing the Song of the Oriole, though shorn from its original story. They do not consider whether it is true or not, for it is just a song to them. And many can tell the tale of the Flock of the Lion but do not believe it. Even the clams of the shallows of Sian Ka'an can tell it, but their tight, sealed shells prevent the pearl it could produce in them."

"I know because of the air you bring to my branches," the allthorn said. "Your aroma subdues my thorns. My leaves, though small, feel a life flowing through them that invigorates them as if I were a palm tree ripe with fruit. And I remember my name because of this. For my kind was there in the Garden—yes, we were. Though in that day, we were tender plants bedecked with flowers delicate and fragrant: the allbloom—so was the name that Eve, the beloved of Adam, gave us. We have not forgotten. Our thorns contain the memory of the bloom, for so the Maker willed it. This is why I know who you are. You are of the Flock of the Lion. You remember Eden."

Oracle looked at the horizon to the north. He perceived something beyond the place where the earth met the sky.

"Yes, I do remember," he said. "So it is doubly good that I answer Kahoo's prayer. For much more than the Lonely Tree is lonely in the Valley. The animals must remember their names."

"Breathe on them, sire, and they will remember what Adam said at the naming of their kind."

"And when they remember," Oracle reflected, "they will become who they should be, so that whether they live or die, the Valley will lead them to high mountain pastures."

"Yes, royal one," the allthorn affirmed. And sacred silence took the center of the conversation again. A quail called in the distance. A flock of sparrows engulfed them for a blink of an eye as it flew north, the birdwings bursting the air with a flutter of passing whispers.

"I desire to see the Lady River," Oracle purred. "How is the way between here and the Great River of the North?"

"The way is arduous, split by bands of molten earth now hardened. Manplaces cluster like crowds of beehives, and sting as much too—at times even with the sting of Death to many of four feet who would pass by them. It will take one full moon from now to reach it."

"Are there dense places of trees and brush?" asked Oracle. "If I have these, it will be well. There is always an invisible way as long as there is a thicket."

"Yes, there are thickets, but they are often cut asunder with farms and fences of ironthorn. However, once you reach the Valley, the offspring of the great Lady River will help you: the crescent lakes and ponds of her pretamed days. Man calls them *resacas*. They refuse to faint before this drought, preserving their water for the egret and the fish. They help the animals travel through places thick with Man, since gardens of my more luxuriant kin grow thick about them."

"Thank you," said Oracle.

"I am honored," said the tree.

"Farewell, oh allthorn, Tree Who Remembers," Oracle said. And he blessed the tree:

May the sunshine give you greenery
May the moonlight give you dew
May your broad arms shelter many
May your years be like the yew.

And the allthorn blessed the jaguar:

Plant the seed that doubles
Plant the seed that grows
Out of Garden stubbles
Grows a thornless rose.

* * *

On the night of the August full moon, Oracle reached the Rio Grande. The way had been arduous, just as the allthorn had warned. Twice a posse of men had chased him, but each time the earth had helped him with a cave whose galleries afforded narrow passages to ways of escape unknown to the hunters.

Oracle found a cattle range whose ironthorn of barbed wire leaned with rusty fatigue. He passed carefully through it. Soon after, he caught the faint scent of the river. At last he reached her southern bank. The trees at the water's edge were half dry and half green, and each one seemed to hold a secret it would never tell. Before him, on the other side, was a curious sight: a great, white barrier of concrete, what the animals called "manstone." Atop the wall ironthorn shone like a coiling serpent armed with razors. Above them a bank of lights hissed from the noise of the elements burning within them. They cast a shimmer upon the surface of the river. Oracle rejoiced to see her.

"Hail, Lady River, heart of the Valley!" he whispered with joy. "I greet you!"

"And I greet you," the river said. "Welcome to the Valley, sire. It is kind of you to come."

"And kind of you to sparkle," Oracle replied. "Thank you for throwing the light into my eyes."

"Sparkle is all that remains of me," said the river. "For the summer rains did not come, and Man has become very thirsty. He has bled me dry. Soon I shall run out of strength altogether, and the beach of the Gulf will close my mouth to aid me. He will hold back my brother the sea, and I will rest."

"Yes," said Oracle. "Man is thirsty, and the heavens are grieved. Between these two things, you have become almost a ghost. But not quite, for your sparkle shows that there is life, and therefore hope."

Oracle traveled along the south bank until he spied a gap in the barrier across the water. Man had heaped earth there, but it was clearly open. And the tracks of a manmachine were discernable like two long, parallel paths that snaked over it and through brittle grass. A halogen lamp hummed above the road, shining on a thickly wooded place that stood beyond it.

Oracle spoke.

"Lady River, I desire to cross you. I must answer the call of the last jaguar, Kahoo the Grave, who perished at the Lonely Tree seventy springs ago. I cross in search of that tree, and I go to help the animals remember the names Adam gave them in the days of Eden. Would you permit me the honor of crossing your waters?"

"Yes, you may," said the Lady River. "With joy I say so, for your crossing is a welcome and brotherly kiss to me. Long has it been since I have drenched the rosette spots of the jaguar. Mingle with me for a moment on your quest that I might remember the last Lord of the Valley and greet the new."

"Lord of the Valley? Is that the name the jaguar goes by here?"

"Yes, it is the name. But no one has walked in that name for seventy springs. It is the stewards who rule in his place."

"Tell me about the stewards," Oracle said, but at that moment the low growl of a distant motor met his ears. Soon after came the scents of boat fuel and burning tobacco. He crouched to hide, bending to blend his spots with the leaves of black mangroves that hid all but his eyes. From downriver came a shallow draft boat marked with a thick, green stripe. It carried two Men. One searched the river with a bright beam.

The boat passed and with it the scent of the fuel, though the aroma of the tobacco remained, burning from some unseen place on the dark shores—a scent of Cuban soil and cloud-rich air.

Oracle emerged from the mangroves. He bowed and touched his lips to the river's surface. He drank her in. He descended into the water, and the Lady River lifted him, causing him to glide with such smoothness that no ripple shimmered or betrayed the motion of his paws in the soothing heart of the river below.

He emerged, dripping and refreshed. But he did not shake off the water, for quietness was the only companion he could take with him through the gap in the manstone.

Oracle turned and bowed to the river.

"Thank you." He purred. "I will return to run beside your bank once I have found the Lonely Tree. I will bring friends who remember their names. Until then, farewell."

"You are welcome," the Lady River whispered. "Fare thee well on thy quest. May you find friends to guide you to the tree:

Be they humble or high wing
Be they cloven or clawed
Be they two-legged who can sing
Be they four-legged who plod

Be it Man the Forgetter
Be it Man though he sleeps

Be it Man breaking fetters
Be it Man who us keeps.

"Find the Lonely Tree, and may you help the animals remember their names along the way. Then return and romp along my banks and meanwhile greet my offspring, the resacas of my ancient paths. All kinds of life gather to them. All kinds. Rejoice in their waters, but do so with open eyes, for not all kinds are *kind*. Even so, my children will provide a way for you through the manplaces."

"Thank you," said Oracle. "You confirm the words of the allthorn tree, who said that such would be so: a watery way through the dry."

Oracle heard a vehicle approaching alongside the manstone. He turned and disappeared into the thick brush, beyond the reach of the halogen lamp. All that remained was the smell of the tobacco leaves, invisible to both the lamp and the searchlights of the Men in their green-striped machines.

* * *

True to the advice of the allthorn and the river, the resacas helped Oracle. "Come," their scent beckoned. "We form a curvy path through the square places where Man lives. Follow us." And so Oracle did—now wading, now walking, now swimming, now wading again, now crouching among the reeds at the sound of Man passing nearby in his machines. Oracle emerged from each resaca searching for the next, moving silently across the grassy slope between one oxbow lake and another, or finding a tunnel through the branches of bushes.

And just as the Lady River had told Oracle, he found that all kinds of life had gathered at the resacas, life as noble as the kin of the monarch butterfly: the many-colored clans of the House of Lepidoptera.

Oracle passed under a footbridge and crept through thick cattails to the bank of a new resaca. The bank was muddy and full of the tracks of those who had come and gone earlier in the night. The sky shone a faint, illumined haze on a great swath of its horizon because of the manplaces that were nearby. From that light, Oracle found that he was at the narrow end of a long resaca that curved slowly away into the dark and wooded distance.

"Another good path," said Oracle. He descended into the water and swam.

Two eyes watched. Eyes upon a gnarled and frowning head. Eyes set in a body fourteen feet long. Eyes set above a jaw with eighty teeth and a pallid tongue. The beast's heavy tail swayed slowly back and forth beneath the smooth surface. No limb moved. But the beast came forward to the middle of the resaca as if drawn toward Oracle by an inexorable gravity.

The alligator spoke to himself.

"What is this?" he whispered. "What threat? What thief? What plunderer with fur? Intruder strange. I know it not."

Oracle saw what appeared to be a log or fallen tree ahead of him in the water.

"Strange branch," he thought, "for it moves as if a river current drives it. But this is no stream. And this log is no lifeless thing. The waters of Sian Ka'an have such branches. I know them."

As Oracle drew closer, the deadwood turned so that its narrow end faced him. Two points glistened on either side of the great, dull tree.

Oracle stopped, and as he did he saw the deadwood bare a row of teeth.

"Who are you?" it said in a low but threatening tone.

"I am the jaguar Oracle of Sian Ka'an."

"Why are you here?" the alligator asked.

"I answer the prayer of Kahoo, the last Lord of the Valley, who called to the moon and stars for a successor seventy springs ago. I explore this unknown realm that I inherit from my distant kin. I search for the Lonely Tree."

"Ha!" spat the alligator. "The Lonely Tree! I know that tale, for the head of my house keeps it. He keeps it and *laughs*, for it will never come to pass."

"Who is the head of your house, and who are you?" asked Oracle.

The beast took in air, inflating himself as he did, to give the answer.

"I am Ghast, son of Grogg, of the House of Reptilia. Grogg is the one who glories in this tale, for in this story is the extinguishing of the long reign of the Lord of the Valley. In his place are cats who skulk like runts, while we, in our cold blood, grow strong. We never go on pilgrimage but remained fixed, immovable in whatever pond we find ourselves, only moving when hunger or a larger relative compels us. But no one is larger than Grogg, and no one has moved him. No wildcat, no coyote, no cougar. Not even Man, the Accursed One. And no one will move *me*. Now turn and go back the way you came."

"I cannot go back once I have put my paw forward," Oracle answered. "This is the direction I must go."

Ghast grunted a long murmur of dismay.

"No Lord of the Valley has crossed this resaca since before the time I hatched on its oozy bank. Leave me in peace. Go away!"

"I will go, but forward, not away."

"Why do you disturb my peace?"

"Maybe your peace needs disturbing."

"Disturbing?" Ghast raised his voice. "You will find my teeth even more so."

"Try and I will pierce your head," said the jaguar.

"Try and I will make you dead!" threatened Ghast. "I own the water of this pond. I forbid you passage. Now go and find another place to lick off your mud."

"For too long have you been left alone, it seems," growled Oracle. "You have come to think you own this pond. But I know that is not true: the tracks around it show that many share it, for all living things have thirst in common. You do not own this resaca."

"Of course I own it!" Ghast snarled as he came closer. "I have lived here all my life! I retreat before no one and run off whom I will. I send the thirsty away thirsty when I find them. This is why I own it; its name and mine are one and the same. This is Ghast's Grotto, and I am *Ghast*! That is my *name*!" And he let off an open-mouthed hiss as he turned the water behind him into a rolling boil with his writhing tail.

Oracle did not move. He considered the small, scum-glazed eyes of the beast.

"Ghast is the name you gave yourself," said Oracle, "but it is not the only name you were given. We all have other names, too, and those names come from the one who is master over us."

"*Master* over us?" Ghast gloated. "*Master*?" And he pressed his cocking head against the jaguar's until Ghast's left eye faced Oracle with no more distance between them than what a moth could pass though. "Who is master over me? I know of no one."

Oracle leveled the gaze of his beryl-green eyes upon the beady stare of the alligator. The stench of the beast hit him harder than he had expected, for it reminded him that he was a stranger in this land and far from the Yucatán, with no ally from his tribe to help him. His gaze wavered; he blinked as his pupils changed from round to narrow to round again in the hypnotic coercion of the reptile's eye. Then Oracle recalled Eden. He spoke.

"Ghast, did you birth yourself?" he asked. "Were you one with the clay of this pond bottom once, proclaiming, 'I will emerge from the mud. I will grow teeth and hide. I will become Ghast, a terror to fish and a bane to fur'?"

"I am my own, you cat," roared Ghast, though his eye now felt dissolved in the beryl green of his adversary's. "My own, you hear! This needs no explaining or thinking. Now fight, that I might tear and crush you. Try your claws on my armor, if you dare. In vain will you find a place to pierce me. And while you do, I will hold you down, cut you open, and skin you alive! I will leave you skinless, and

I will wear your spotted coat like a muddy robe on my back while you wander about the flatlands naked and howling. You will never try to seize me again! Then all will hear and leave me alone—even Man, the Accursed One."

He descended into the water, and the Lady River lifted him.

CHAPTER 5

A BENT BUT LIVING WORLD

ORACLE dove. In that eyeblink moment between the cat's unexpected move and Ghast coming to himself, the jaguar reached the base of the beast's tail. Up the cat shot as Ghast plunged down. Teeth sank into the alligator's tail. With Oracle now firmly fixed in the reptile's flesh, Ghast found that every move he made toward the cat actually thrust him away. In vain the alligator snapped his jaws at empty water. Then Oracle flung himself, claw after claw, up the side and then the back of the thrashing beast until he was squarely above Ghast's shoulders. The claws found the soft places around Ghast's eyes, and Oracle set them there just short of the depth that brings pain. Ghast reared his head to toss the cat, but Oracle set his fangs like a pincer on the base of Ghast's skull. The teeth pressed upon, though not quite through, the tender place between the armor of the animal's head and back. Ghast opened his jaws. Clouded, green water drained off a death-colored maw through a toothy sieve, but the cat was beyond their reach.

Ghast rolled. The farther he moved into the roll, the tighter the jaguar's claws and fangs pushed upon the beast's rugged hide, until, with Oracle fully underwater and upside down, the jaguar's teeth and claws just reached the nerves and veins of the coldblood.

Ghast gasped. He rolled himself aright and forbade himself to inhale more air than necessary, fearing the inflation of his body would be all that was needed for Oracle to snap the cord of life within him.

Oracle spoke. "I do not want to kill you," he whispered through his teeth, "for you have many years and many choices yet to make in the secret place beneath your thick skin. But if you decide to fight on, it will be the last choice you make. You will sink to the bottom of this pond, and your carrion will become food for the catfish and the turtle."

Ghast glared around him with his baleful eyes, but he could see nothing but the paws of his possessor, whose claws, like jail bars, intruded on his dim line of sight whichever way he looked. Slowly he moved to the far shore of the resaca until he was alongside it. Oracle released his grip, but he did not disembark. Instead, he breathed the memory of Eden on Ghast.

The alligator felt a strange new air about him. The breath passed over his head like a cool breeze preceding the rain. His anger also cooled, and with it the sense of threat from Oracle's fangs. The breath lingered over Ghast, settled, and sank through his calloused hide. The alligator closed his jaws. Oracle hopped ashore.

"Why did you not kill me?" Ghast whispered.

"Because you still have life," said Oracle. "It is a bent life in a bent world, but life nonetheless. As long as one has life, there is hope."

The beast looked at the cat, and as he did his vision became clearer, his eyes silver with the slit-lamp sharpness of his younger days. In the glow of the full moon, Ghast saw how gently the jaguar's spotted coat shone and how the white trim of his mouth and body reflected a color for which there was no word—a clear blue that was dark but bright, a cool radiance that penetrated the beholder and made a home in him. And the sight of Oracle, together with the cool breath, caused a memory to awaken, the memory of a name. It was a name Ghast had not heard before, yet it aroused a chorus of joy within his armored frame—a shout that the name rightly belonged to him. And suddenly it seemed to the alligator that the name "Ghast" had not really been his name at all, but more like the thin skin of a grape, which, bursting from the ripeness of something far better, revealed another name in its place—sweet and full and rich. And with the name came a story. Ghast remembered it from that day until the last sunset he saw, many years later, when, beyond the sunset, it was no longer a memory but alive.

* * *

There was a time in Eden when the waters danced with the moonlight, and when they did, the waddling folk could not easily cross with their offspring. The little ones, unaccustomed to the aquatic dance, would get caught in the swirling joy and separated from their mothers. With much commotion they would reunite, but the baby birds were fragile and hard-pressed to reach the other side.

There was a certain creature in the pond who danced with the roots of the cypress and the mangrove, for he resembled a root, with long tail and stump-like limbs and skin of strange variation. He noticed the trouble of the ducklings.

"Have them climb on my back," he said to their mothers. "It is broad enough for them to rest on, and its knobs and bumps will not permit them to slip."

The creature brought his large body to the edge of the water, where the mother ducks gently prodded their offspring to board. The mothers swam alongside the creature while he ferried their young across. The ducklings rested and quietly murmured a tune in harmony with the ripples of the pond and the frogs on the shore. And so in this way, by the light of the moon and through the dancing waters, the little ones safely crossed to the other side. Broad was the smile the creature gave in his delight.

A curious quail, who watched from the cypress branches, flew to Adam and told him what had happened. Adam went to the water and watched the following night how the creature, though ungainly on land, gracefully ferried the little ones to safety through the dancing waters.

"*Hospitalis* is your name," he said, "for you are a friend to strangers."

And Adam sang this song to him:

The Host not hostile
The mouth is docile
The Fear is fading
For young birds wading

The beast befriending
To make an ending
Of troubled waters
For sons and daughters.

* * *

Inside of Ghast, the song continued for what seemed to him to be the length of seven summers, though only a moment passed. Then it ended. Ghast lingered in the aroma of the tale, lying in it as placidly as his body lay at rest in the resaca. He spoke.

"I remember now. Yes, I remember what he said to the first of my kind."

"You remember," said Oracle.

"Yes. Somehow your breath did it." The alligator savored the memory in silence. "Thank you. I am a guest of this resaca and now a grateful one. Therefore, Guest is who I am and Ghast no longer."

And he spoke this poem to Oracle:

A grateful guest
Should not deny

His fellow guest
To cross the pond

For now I know
That you and I
Are henceforth bless'd
With special bond.

Oracle bowed to the guardian of the resaca and bid the quiet beast farewell.

The alligator Guest watched the jaguar Oracle depart, calm and strong, into a leafy veil of mangrove and willow.

* * *

By way of sleeping manpaths and a maze of hedges, Oracle reached the next resaca. There grew the oldest and tallest surviving tree from the days before the manmachines had plowed the forest under: a Montezuma cypress with sprawling roots and towering boughs and long, branchy, moss-bedecked leaves hanging like the mantles of kings.

The cypress greeted Oracle.

"Welcome, Cat of the Rosette Spots. A long winter it has been since the last Lord of the Valley walked here, a winter of seventy springs. Hail to you."

"And hail to you, oh Ancient Sage. May I rest under your branches? I am weary from hosting an unexpected guest."

"Gladly, sire, come and rest."

Oracle reclined alongside the broad trunk of the cypress. "Tell me about this land," he said. "For I am from the wetlands of a place far from here, Sian Ka'an of the Yucatán, and I have not trodden this way before. I am in search of the Lonely Tree where the last jaguar called for one like me. And I am here to help the animals remember their names."

"Ah yes, Kahoo the Grave was his name," said the cypress. "I knew him. He marked my bark with his noble paw as a sign of his rule. I was his resting place in the heat of the day."

"Tell me what you know about Kahoo," Oracle said.

"He was the offspring of a rugged tribe in the mountains of the south," the cypress said. "He lived in the days before the raising of the Great Barrier that now blocks the way between that realm and this one. News reached Kahoo that the paw of the jaguar had grown faint in the Valley. He crossed the river to strengthen it, though many a jaguar had warned him that the paths of the cats had grown too narrow in this place. But he crossed the Lady River and did not turn back. He gathered the cats of the Valley—jaguar, ocelot, bobcat, jaguarundi, and wandering cougar—a Council of the Cats. Through brave deeds he won their loyalty. From then until his death, Kahoo conferred with them for counsel, and in the Sanctuary of Sabal Palms, he would hold court—the Court of the Animals it was called. There, he would mete out decisions just and fair. After each court he would greet the Lady River, walking the green band of life along her banks until he reached the beach where her waters met her brother the sea. In that place he would kiss the Lady River. He would swim her water at her mouth and rejoice at the place where earth, sky, and water—both fresh and salt—hold constant, pleasant conversation, a place Man calls *Boca Chica*.

"But all that came to an end. Man, whom the cypresses call the Tribe of the Anxious Eye, removed the remnant race of rosette spots until only Kahoo remained. Man overtook him as he paced his realm in one final search for his fellow jaguars. It happened in the top of the Lonely Tree."

"Where is that tree?" Oracle asked.

"North of here, within a half moon's travel, I surmise, but whether northeast or northwest or due north, I do not know. The bards who keep the memory of Kahoo alive do not say. But the quail, who sing among my branches each year, recite his prayer. Even while I sleep they sing it, and when they sing, I dream the words."

"This is what the last jaguar said. In his final moment, Kahoo cried out to heaven:

Oh moon, hear!
Oh stars, listen to me!
I depart the earth this night to join my fathers,
But you remain, and you keep watch.
Do not leave this river delta bare.
Do not leave it unled forever.
Watch in my place, and wait with open eyes
Until another comes to lead the kingdom
From the north and from the sky,
From here to river's end!

The cypress paused in silent meditation after he had chanted these words. A breeze from the sea whispered through his leaves. The moonlight, reaching down through the branches, moved back and forth over Oracle in a pattern of spots that were her own.

"The river delta is no longer bare, for a jaguar is now present," Oracle said. "But since I do not come 'from the north and from the sky,' as Kahoo prayed, I cannot tell how the prophecy will come to pass. Perhaps I am to go north and find a jaguar to bring here."

"None of your kind are there," replied the cypress, "for it is the realm of the cougar, not the jaguar. It has been that way for an age. As long as I have had roots in this soil, this has been the northernmost place in the animal kingdom where jaguars ruled."

"Tell me," Oracle asked, "who now rules the animal kingdom here in the place of the jaguar? The Lady River told me of the stewards, and another rough and recent friend called them skulking cats. Who are they?"

"The ocelot and the bobcat are the stewards of the Valley," said the cypress. "They are the remnant of the Cats of the Three Tribes. Alas, the jaguarundi has vanished, and the cougar has lost his way. Only two tribes are left. These are the only ones who remain from the Council of the Cats that the Lord of the Valley hosted. But in the jaguar's absence, the moon does not shine on our nights in the same way, nor do our days bloom strong in the sun. The ocelot and the bobcat rule with faint hearts, for their kinds are vanishing here too. This is why your rough friend called them skulking cats."

"Where do they meet?"

"They do not meet," the cypress replied. "There has been no Council of the Cats since Kahoo. Only the two surviving stewards confer with one another, and their place of counsel is secret."

"Who are they?"

"Pace the ocelot and Force the bobcat. But they do not live in their names. The coyotes run roughshod over the land, and the cougar who passes through has no ruler over him but joins the vagabond ghosts of Man to frighten the living."

Oracle contemplated what he had heard. He let the silence flood in, pregnant with unspoken words. A quail sang in the distance.

"I have a clear path to follow now," said Oracle. "I know what I must do. I will find the Lonely Tree. I will call a Council of the Cats. I will hold court in the Sanctuary of Sabal Palms, the Court of the Animals, to mete out decisions, just and fair. I will tell the story of the Lion of Gihon Isle. I will breathe the air of Eden on whosoever will bend the neck to receive it. And they shall remember what Adam spoke to them. Yes, they will remember their names."

"If you do these things," said the cypress, "then the paw of the jaguar will have made a path for many others, though his own paw may fade."

"Both the path and the paw are under the hand of Man," Oracle said. "He is the one who will set the boundary lines on these things, for his choices create mine."

Then Oracle chanted a song, swaying gently, not unlike what the lion had done in the dream of the banana tree in the Yucatán:

I'll counsel cats
Restore the court
I'll cause to bloom
The August tree

I'll kiss the stream
Console her hurt
I'll see what Man
Will choose for me:

To throw the net
And drag me back
Or call me free
To prowl and track

Or take my life
As trophy won
And send me far
Behind the sun.

There was silence. The stars sang. The wind translated the tune into a hush heard only in the heart. Oracle leaned against the tree.

"Farewell, oh cypress, Tree of Kings," he said.

"Farewell, oh Path Maker," the cypress replied, and he blessed the jaguar:

Swim the lake and find the star
That never turns but beckons far
And see which way that Man will guide
Through narrow gates or prairies wide

To find the path and climb the tree
And tell the sky it's been set free
From watching years of vigilance
And waiting moons of starry dance
No longer named a Lonely Tree
No longer lonely, you and me.

"Thank you," said Oracle. "You have spoken a map to me." And he scratched his mark on the bark of the tree, a scar the cypress bore gladly.

CHAPTER 6

THE FRIEND

ORACLE reached a deep resaca in the watery trail he had followed since kissing the Lady River. A stand of black willows formed a curtained pavilion overhanging the water. Oracle rested beneath them, watching and listening as the cricket song gave way to dawn. Oracle slept. The weariness of his nine-month journey began to melt away. At midday he awakened. A flock of whistling ducks landed on the lake. Oracle lay just beyond their sight under the willows. He watched the flock enjoy the resaca with the nervous alertness of their kind—swimming and pruning and resting but never forgetting to pensively survey their world or call to one another with the whistle of their tribe, one that mixed joy and anxious thought in equal measure. In the afternoon Oracle contemplated a turtle performing his silent meditations on the barkless branch of an old, fallen tree, half sunk in the water. At length night returned, the moon rising with eager curiosity to see the cat with the rosette spots, the new Lord of the Valley.

Oracle heard someone on the opposite shore. He searched for the source of the sound. There it was: a small, bearlike creature in a furtive pose, dipping something in and out of the water. Oracle noiselessly slipped into the lake and out from the veil of willow leaves. Silently he moved across the resaca toward the cub, or whatever it was, on the far shore.

The little animal was too delighted with the object of his washing to notice the approaching predator. He had caught a fiddler crab and was preparing it for supper. He was just beginning to remove the spindly parts of the creature when, through the crook in the crab's greater claw (the one called a fiddle), he spied a behemoth he had never seen before. He dropped his paws, but he remained mindful of clutching the crab, who brandished his fiddle claw at his captor with fearsome threats. The holder of the crab, however, was not aware of those threats, for he stood speechless as the great thing in the water moved closer and grew larger.

Patch the raccoon considered what to do as the great cat rose dripping before him. It was ten times his weight and four times his size. The crab, who didn't give a shell for the new, giant, spotted thing that dripped before him, clubbed the raccoon's paw.

"W-would you care for a crab?" asked Patch.

"No, thank you," replied Oracle. "You have hunted it, and it is yours to eat."

"But perhaps you should eat it," the raccoon insisted delicately. "Then other things are less likely to be eaten."

"I have always preferred fish to fur," Oracle said.

"Well, then, you've come to the right place!" said Patch, in a volume carried higher than necessary by a wave of relief. "This resaca's full of your favorites! There's molly and buffalo and blue-spotted tilapia. Mullet are everywhere, and now and then a bass passes through! And if you're hungry enough to do battle for your meal, then the sharp-toothed garfish will give you both. Why, some are as heavy as you are, I'm told…Um, by the way, sire, who are you?"

"I am the jaguar Oracle," he said. "I come from a distant place called Sian Ka'an in the manrealm called the Yucatán."

"You're traveling north, I take it?" asked Patch.

"Yes, that is the ruling direction for me," replied Oracle. "I seek the Lonely Tree and all the roots it leads to in the Valley."

The jaguar looked deep into the eyes of the raccoon. "And who, may I ask, are you?"

Patch gulped, but it was hard to swallow. "I beg your pardon, but I'm reluctant to say. Not all are friends with my kind, sire, and, according to our ways, we decline to make our presence known, lest paws and pellet guns find difficulty in being friendly with us."

"Well, if you're reluctant to tell me your kind, at least tell me your name," said Oracle.

"I've been given many names, sire. I've been called Robber of Nest Eggs and Hatcher of Pranks. Trickster, huckster, slacker, shirker. A trapper waiting to be trapped. A hat waiting to be made. The Algonquin mantribe calls us, 'He Who Scratches with His Hands.' The dwellers in the manplaces call me pest. I like the Algonquin name better."

"Do all your acquaintances call you these names?" Oracle asked.

"Oh, not all," the raccoon replied. "Some just call me Patch— oops! Ha! Silly me! Yes, that's my name. Pace the ocelot calls me that, and so does Force the bobcat. They're the stewards of the Valley. I carry messages for them across the manrealms to the scattered members of their tribes. I'm known to Swog the javelina, and he calls me Patch too. The coyotes don't call me anything, but at the same time, I have no enemies among them. Sometimes, the best way to have no enemies is to be called nothing."

"And where does my nameless fisherman named Patch hail from?"

"I am from the manplace called Palo Verde Estates, a two-night journey from here. It's got plenty of hiding places near the resacas, and there are plenty of treasures to borrow."

"Borrow?"

"Yes!" Patch replied. "Man has so much that he generously shares it. He leaves ways open for me to collect what he has lost track of."

"I am sure you have quite a collection of treasures Man has lost track of," Oracle commented.

"Oh yes, indeed I have," replied Patch, and his eyes brightened in their black mask. But then, as if puzzled by a question posed to himself, he frowned and furrowed his brow and, in his introspection, inadvertently dropped his guard again. "Some say we raccoons are good at *burgling*, but we always say we're good at *borrowing*. For nothing's really ours, you know, or yours. I mean no offense to say so, sire, but sooner or later another enjoys what you gather, and lastly the sea or the soil or the air takes it back. And yes, I admit, our clan has its secrets on how to borrow, one for each ring on our tails."

"We jaguars have rings on our tails, too," Oracle said, "but they are not just for recording our secrets. They're for fishing."

"Fishing?" asked Patch as he cocked his head.

"Here, I'll show you," the jaguar said, and he reclined along the grassy bank with his forepaws casually drooping at the water's edge like an aloof Persian cat on the arm of a couch. Oracle extended his tail over the surface of the water and dropped its tip downward. The tip, bordered by the last ring of the cat's tail, hovered just above the surface. The jaguar looked at the reflection of the fair disc of the moon floating on the gray-blue water. As Oracle did so, now and then a drop of saliva from his open mouth fell onto the pond, leaving a curious shape on the surface.

In the aquatic world below, fish looked up to see a fascinating sight. Outlined by the light of the moon, a shadowy thing like a moth hovered just above the gossamer film of the water's surface, while nearby a fleet of tiny shapes like water striders drifted along the surface itself. Allured by this enigma, a fish approached to investigate.

Whap!

The once-docile paws flashed and flipped a fish to the shore—a stunned, striped mullet.

Patch's eyes widened with amazement. He dropped the crab, who scuttled away with a parting glare toward fish and fur.

"You may have it," said Oracle. "I'll catch another for myself." And after a moment, he did—this time a tilapia.

By the time the moon's reflection had moved to the edge of the resaca's mirroring surface, both the jaguar and the raccoon were full of fish. Oracle placed his tail over the water for one last morsel for Patch.

Deep within the resaca, a garfish in his drainpipe lair had become very irritated with the incessant splashes and chatter of swimming things above him. Out from the pipe he probed with his long, tooth-filled jaw, which in shape resembled the alligator's so much that Man had nicknamed him the alligator gar. He steamed toward the place where he heard the noises. There he spied the faux moth and phantom water striders, but gars are too ornery to be charmed. He lunged straight out of the water and chomped the jaguar's tail.

Oracle flinched and flung his paws over the fish as both rolled into the resaca, but the gar only clamped down harder. Underwater, the jaguar and the gar twisted in a swirl of gurgling bubbles until Oracle closed his jaws over the back of the fish. Oracle's teeth struggled through the squirming scales of the beast, who kicked back like an angry, living cowboy boot. But the cat's teeth prevailed, finding the vertebrae and snapping them as if they were stubborn hackberry branches.

With rivulets flowing from his coat, Oracle emerged from the resaca, dragging the gar behind him, the postmortem meanness of his jaws still locked onto the jaguar's tail. Oracle looked back at the mangled devil.

"Oh my!" Patch said. "Let me help you." The thought of how much the needle teeth of the gar must hurt made Patch forget his fear of the king-size carnivore. He hobbled up to the gar's carcass and used the claw on the end of each digit of his forepaws to wheedle his way between the gar fangs. Once all his digits were lodged between them, he pulled the jaws until they popped open. Patch heaved aside the lifeless, gaping thing and dipped Oracle's tail up and down in the water.

"Let me clean this better," Patch said. The raccoon hurried to a small rise of ground a stone's throw down shore, where a patch of pita plants grew. He pulled one up and returned. Oracle watched as the raccoon beat the pita's soapy essence to the surface of the roots and then smeared it on the jaguar's tail.

"I'll fetch some aloe vera for you," Patch told Oracle after he had finished bathing the wounds. "It will heal quite well that way."

"Thank you," said Oracle.

Patch returned in the early morning with fresh fronds of the aloe vera. Scooping out its gel, he applied the balm to the jaguar's wounds.

"How soothing," commented Oracle. "Where did you find it?"

"At a manplace where many pots of aloe vera grow," said Patch. "The boss of that manplace always lets me borrow them and snack a bit on morsels. In fact, I brought back a snack for *you*. Here!" Patch offered Oracle a curiously shaped tidbit with an odd odor of fish and factory lubricants. Oracle involuntarily crinkled his nose.

"What is it?" he asked.

"It's called cat food," Patch announced with glee. "I heard the people of the manplace say it. They keep this for little cousins of yours—the felines who live with them. The people in one manplace are so eager to share it with me that they even placed a small flap in their kitchen door so that I can freely come and go! They often leave a whole dish of cat food for me to borrow. Would you like me to get more?"

"No, thank you," said Oracle, whose tongue compelled a frown as he chewed the morsel, though in the chewing, the frown did not look obvious. "I am still full from the night's catch."

"OK," said Patch. "Just let me know when you'd like me to borrow more for you."

Fireflies arrived over the water. For a space of time, the raccoon and the jaguar watched them in their aerial dance of hide-and-seek—a secret, silent semaphore that could only be understood if a soul became very, very still. The lake faded into a moonless, clear, gray sky as the sun prepared to rise.

"Where are the treasures you have borrowed?" Oracle asked. "Are they far from here? You must be worried that someone may take them while you take care of me."

"Oh, they are not far," Patch replied with a singing lilt. "And they are well hidden. There is only one treasure I *really* worry about."

"Which one is that?" Oracle asked.

"The one called marbles," he said, and his eyes widened as if he were an explorer from Panama describing the newfound Pacific Ocean. "Marbles are my dearest treasure. To lose them would be worse than losing anything else I have ever borrowed—than everything else put together. I'm fine to show them and to lend them, but to lose them—ah, that would leave me with an empty den!"

"An empty den?" Oracle asked.

"The treasures are all I've got," Patch replied.

"No family?"

"No, not yet. I mean, sure, we raccoons have as many cousins as the hackberry has leaves, but what you call an honest-to-goodness *family*, nope. Don't have one. I'd like to, but I'm busy with my treasures. Gotta keep 'em organized and outta sight of the ravens. In time, I guess. In time I'll have a family."

Oracle pondered what Patch had said. He noticed the glow of the sun's first rays on the raccoon's furry back, though Patch himself could not see it.

Patch turned and scampered off without a farewell. After a few moments, he returned with dust on his nose and a pouch in his paws. He fished out a series of marbles—six in all—setting each one down reverently in a group before Oracle. The rays of the morning sun pierced the orbs and threw a cluster of stars on the ground, each one ensconced in an oval shadow. And inside each marble hovered a three-tongued flame of colors. Patch rolled a marble back and forth between his forepaws. Then he held it up to a sunbeam that traversed it, and he gazed into the marble as if he were espying a planet through a telescope.

Oracle drew near, and Patch saw him from the corner of his eye. He sensed an imminent presence with the jaguar, not visible but there, as when a whale watcher knows that a rare, mammoth blue is beneath his boat, even though he has not yet seen it. The sense of its being there is as weighty as the thing itself.

Patch's eyes remained fixed on the marble, but now more out of fear for what he might find when he turned them toward Oracle than fascination with the glass ball. For the presence that accompanied Oracle loomed ever larger, eclipsing Patch's thoughts as when the earth eclipses the moon on those special, select evenings of the stars when destinies are determined.

"Patch," said Oracle, and he paused to drink in joy. "Come."

Patch gathered his strength. First he lifted his eyes above the marble and into the morning light. It was all he could do to keep from shaking. Then he faced Oracle.

"Sire," Patch said, the word struggling to travel through his dry mouth. "You come from a line of kings. I come from a line of thieves." And his nose throbbed to hold back tears.

"Welcome, Fair Bandit," said Oracle.

The raccoon drew near the jaguar and bowed before him. Oracle, the Lord of the Valley, quietly told Patch the story of Adam naming the animals. He told how Adam had given them each a voice with a unique word known only to the one who heard it. Then Oracle breathed on Patch. And the air of Eden came, melting away generations of isolation and misunderstanding, of fear and suspicion, of greed and gluttony. And He Who Scratches with His Hands, as the Algonquin had named him, remembered what the father of all

Algonquin and every other mantribe had named his first ring-tailed ancestor in the Garden of Eden—before the Tree of Life vanished, and all wandered into the wilderness alone.

The jaguar and the raccoon were full of fish.

CHAPTER 7

THE BOY FROM THE SEA

I N the lavender gray of the same morning that Patch and Oracle were becoming friends, a lone bird kept vigil in the sky. Chalice the Canada goose flew over the nearby coast of the Gulf of Mexico. Flying northward above a lighthouse, she spied below a southbound squadron of brown pelicans patrolling the beach. Chalice noticed they did not fly in their routine formation but had shifted their usual single row into the avian signal of distress.

"What is this?" she asked herself. "The dawn reveals to the pelicans that all is not well."

The goose turned around, descended southward, and overtook them.

"Greetings, Watchers of the Strand," called Chalice. "I wish you peace."

"And you, Watcher of the Lost," replied the lead pelican.

"What news do you have?" Chalice asked. "What have you seen?"

"A boy's body lies silent upon the beach of El Realito Bay," the pelican said.

"Is he alive?" Chalice asked.

"We do not know," the pelican replied. "But another was with him, for when the sky awoke and our eyes first fell upon the boy, a Man sat in the sand beside him, still as stone. Then he rose and trod wearily toward the manplace called Bahia Mar. He has not returned. The seagulls now circle the air above El Realito, calling to one another about the boy from the sea."

Chalice considered what to do. Beneath her passed a causeway that stretched across the waters until it reached a long row of tall manplaces, a resort town known as South Padre Island. Chalice watched as the tops of the towers caught the first rays of dawn.

"Here there are plenty of Men to find a lost boy," she said, "but not at El Realito."

Chalice thanked the pelicans and bade them farewell. Before her, the causeway, the manplaces, and the island dropped away as she rose and turned. Her eyes filled with pale-orange sky. Now heading north again, Chalice saw beneath her the great, long, costal barrier island that met the Texas shore—a bold, sandy stripe called Padre Island, which gently curved seaward with the bend of the coast and disappeared on the horizon. The island changed as she flew. It became less and less the haunt of Man and more and more a place of secrets, a place where the beach whispered toward the sea, where the marsh looked with longing toward the land, and where the silent dunes meditated in between.

The coast of the mainland filled with inlets and coves, at places jutting far out, and at other places welcoming the saltwater far inland to mingle with the fresh. The goose recognized an egg-shaped body of water, Stover Cove by name. At last, before Chalice was El Realito Bay. The earthen arm that created the bay was a spit of land shaped like a breaching whale. A thread of beach connected the whale's tail to the mainland, where it joined a place Man had named Laguna Atascosa. It was there, on that tiny strip of earth, that the pelicans had reported the boy lay. And, just as the pelicans had said, a flock of seagulls hovered over the spot, a shimmering cloud of white wings that obscured the view.

Chalice descended toward the narrow neck of El Realito, whose breadth at first was no wider than the string of sand that descends in an hourglass. Though she could not see much through the flock of seagulls, Chalice could just make out a dot the size of an ant. As she descended, the ant became a sleeping fawn, and then the fawn became a child lying on his right side. Chalice entered the flock of seagulls above the child.

"Greetings, Dancers of the Sky!" called Chalice.

"Greetings, Bird of the North!" replied the lead seagull, whose name was Sand. "What brings you to our Circle of Council?"

"The pelicans have told me that all is not well. A Man has abandoned a manchild. I must attend to things abandoned, for I am from a flock of birds who have lost their mates and their kin. We are the Colony of the Lost. We dwell on Green Island north of here. I am a watcher of the lost."

"We were here first, here first!" countered Sand. "The manchild is our business. We fly in a Circle of Council to decide what to do, to do!"

Chalice turned along with Sand in the swirling flock. "What is there to decide?" she challenged. "Descend now! See if the boy from the sea still has breath! Cry to the manplaces of Bahia Mar, that perhaps someone might come running!"

"In due time, due time!" replied Sand. "But first each gull must have his say, his say! Then we will choose who has the final word, final word!"

Chalice gave the call of her kind in alarm. "The boy himself is the final word! His body and the beach that holds him call to us. Descend with me!"

But the seagulls continued in their aerial whirligig, calling to one another, looking down at the manchild and at each other with a lively chatter so noisy that no single line of thought, let alone a single sentence, was distinguishable.

"When will you finish your council?" Chalice urged.

"No way to tell, to tell!" called Sand. "We must wait till all of us have cried out what we think to do, to do! When in time we all cry the same, the same, then we will know, will know!"

"I cannot wait for you!" Chalice shouted. "The shore and the sand and the sea have summoned us! They present to us a manchild, a son of Man who rules us, and we should not delay!"

"Go your way then," replied Sand. "Do what you must, you must. But if you find trouble, find trouble, we're not to blame! To blame!"

Chalice banked way from the seagulls in frustration. She made a broad descending arc and landed beside the manchild with a small spray of sand from her wings and webbed feet. She announced her arrival with the honking maternal call of her kind. The child lay motionless.

Chalice looked carefully at the boy. He was covered with matted sand. He was dressed in knee-length shorts of a faded navy plaid. His shirt bore thin stripes. Thrown over him was an oil-stained, orange life jacket that covered his back and head. One of the drawstrings lay over the corner of his mouth. Beside the boy was a half-crumpled, half-empty plastic jug. A green cord tied to its handle hung limp and frayed a handbreadth from the boy's palm. The goose took a step closer.

Four dark shadows swooped over Chalice's head in succession and landed in the sand with a parched-throated croak of a greeting to the boy.

"Hail, Dish of the Day! Tasty to 'meat' you! Ha!"

Vultures.

Chalice hissed at them in warning.

"We are here to help," croaked one vulture, whose withered and naked head showed that he was the oldest. "We can move things along for you. The sea has brought us a corpse to clean, and the shore holds it up to us. The manchild will make a good meal."

The vultures lumbered up to Chalice, close enough for the reek of their feathers to sting the goose's senses. Chalice lunged at them.

"Back!" she cried, and the startled birds, though large, retreated a step, giving Chalice a throaty, sickly hiss. They stared her down with one-eyed glares.

"We know death when we see it," the oldest vulture whispered. "Oh yes, our eyes know. If not dead, then soon dead, which is just the same. See to it that you are not soon dead too! Now fly!"

Chalice stretched her body to its full height and flapped a forceful warning.

"You wrongly hasten what you hope for!" she said. "You do not know his state, and you have no right to alter it so that you can eat as you please! *You* fly!"

Chalice snapped at a vulture. Then she leaned her neck low to the ground, stretched her head forward with open beak, wings arched high, and ran hissing at another.

The vultures lifted off the ground in clumsy commotion, only to land right beside the manchild—one at his feet, one on each side, and one at his head. The oldest vulture chuckled a greasy laugh.

"We are four, and you are one," he said. "A single goose should count her foes and accept that four must do what four must do. Let the goose look to her own feathers. The seagulls do, and they are many. They keep their Circle of Council busy because of us. 'Better talk than talons,' they say. Such wise birds!" The old buzzard smiled.

Chalice swept her Canadian wings across the sand and flung it into the eyes of the vultures. Two were blinded for a moment, flinching. The other two hopped back in caution. Chalice grabbed the leg of a half-blinded foe and flipped him with her unrelenting beak as she rose. The oldest vulture struck at her but missed as the goose brought a wing down on his head. Chalice dove onto the sand once more, sending up sting and noise and feathers into the faces of the vultures.

"This kill will be the death of us!" said one. "It takes more strength to fight than the strength we'll get from the corpse of the boy. Not worth the beak and feathers of this dead body's foolish guard, I say! Let us move on to find another gift from the sea. In time our enemy will leave this carcass, and we will sup. The heat of the long day will make the flesh all the sweeter by the time we return. But for now, let us find a meal of lesser effort."

The vultures heaved themselves up into the sky, stocky legs drooping beneath them. They made a series of guttural calls, insults to Chalice and comfort to each other. They flew northeast and grew small in the distance. The seagulls grew silent by the command of Sand, and the birds now flew back and forth above Chalice and the boy in a hover of curiosity.

Chalice drew near the boy from the sea. She spread her wings, which brought a sheltering shadow over the boy's body. Then, between interludes of silence, she gave the trumpet call of a mother searching for her brood. Three times she gave it. In the quiet moment between each call, the shore's gentle sea song abided in the boy's ears, and the gulf breeze gave him her caresses.

The boy felt the end of the life jacket drawstring lying upon his lips. He opened his mouth and let it drop in. He drew in its salt as his tongue moistened.

Chalice saw it, and she sang the song of the cool Canadian spring. Then she turned to the gulf breeze. "Take comfort, wind, and let him breathe you in," she said. "The manchild is alive." And she returned to her watch in the sky.

* * *

While Oracle rested in the midday heat, Patch went exploring. He found a stand of wild mustang vines covering a dwarf ash tree, and the cardinals were not at all pleased that their hoard had been discovered. The raccoon accepted their consternation with meekness and tried to dine anyway. He curled himself over while he ate so that the cardinals only saw his ball of fur and the obscure motion of his head.

"If they do not see the grapes disappearing, maybe they will be less aggravated," he reasoned.

But to the cardinals, the raccoon's posture communicated disrespect. It only drove them to dart about the tangled vines and tree branches more frantically, protesting loudly. Occasionally they swooped low across Patch, buzzing near him as closely as they dared. But they did not peck him, for this was beneath their cardinal dignity. Patch left his unfinished meal hanging on its tangled branches. He saluted a thank-you to the cardinals, hoping that it would be taken as a gesture of acknowledgment that his eating had been a dreadful inconvenience to them, but the cardinals took it for mockery and lifted en masse from the bush into a swirling fury above him. Patch sighed, dropped to all fours, and shuffled into a nearby thicket to lick clean his paws.

Later Patch reached a sugar hackberry tree where he had made his most recent home (for raccoons move from place to place, borrowing the empty dens of others). In the hackberry was a hollow place where he hid his treasures. He stored them in a cloth bag cinched with a maroon cord, a pouch that had once held a bottle of Grey Flannel cologne before its wearer had tossed the pouch and Patch had found it. Patch plunged his paw into the pouch and greeted all that was in it. He touched a cork that had stopped a bottle of Russian River chardonnay. Patch had found the cork on the red-and-white-checkered picnic blanket of lovers too preoccupied with each other's eyes to notice that he had become their guest. Patch liked the smell of the cork. Whenever he sniffed it, he was transported back to the lovers' picnic. And although he had never been to the wine cellars of Sonoma, he went there as well, for the aroma of the oaken barrels in which the wine had aged still lingered in the cork. Then Patch touched a lacquered wooden cross small enough to fit into his paw. A hole had been bored in the sides of its upper end so that it appeared to have been part of a necklace. Patch liked the smell of the cross too. Its cedar scent mixed with the lacquer to take him back to a mysterious place of incense and candles, whose bell tower had afforded him a home for a season. Also in the pouch were three small seashells. One, a common periwinkle, was dark brown and white, with tiny stairs ascending as if spiraling up a miniature tower. Another looked like the toy pinnacle of a building, an ancient ziggurat of patina green and ivory white. The third was the shape of a geisha doll's fan with patterns of black, white, and crab-back red. Patch liked to gather these shells in his paws and move them back and forth, listening to their *click-clack* as they touched one another and as he admired their colors. Also in the pouch were a green satin ribbon and a black shoestring. Rolling about in silence with them was an ornamental leather baseball the size of a walnut with the words *Republica Dominicana* imprinted in a field of blue and red. The ball had been part of a key chain; it had broken away from the ornamental leather glove to which it had been sewn. A part of another keychain was also in the pouch—a tiny cowboy spur with a brass rowel that really worked. There was also a safety pin and the kind of treasure every raccoon covets: shiny buttons. Patch had three: a two-hole, engraved nickel button the size of a dime; a smaller faux diamond with one loop on its back; and a black, four-hole coat button almost as big as a watch face. At last Patch's slender claws clicked in greeting against the marbles. He caressed their faces like treasured friends. His normal vision clouded over, for the vision of the marbles in his mind's eye was more vivid than the sunlit hackberry tree visible to his natural sight.

In this placid moment, Patch heard a step.

He looked with fixed gaze at the green veil before him, but his eyes were only obeying the command of what his ears had heard, knowing full well that they would as yet have nothing to say about the matter.

The noise sounded familiar, like the clumsy thump of Man. Patch leaned into the next round-footed sound; yes, it was Man, all right. However, Patch's ears told him that the step was neither tense nor cautious. The following step even told Patch's ears that the feet of this Man were not intent on a single direction. The vibration of the earth echoed an indistinct path.

"So, it's not a hunter," Patch thought, considering, "but who? And why *here*? Man doesn't hunt for mustang grapes, unless the Man is Grandmother, and, well, this is indeed the time for Grandma's jam and wine. My, the scoops and scoops of sugar she pours in! But this footstep is not the sound of a grown one. It's too light."

Patch moved from his alcove and through the thicket, tracking the footsteps with his ears.

"No scent yet," he whispered to himself. "Wait! There it is! It's Man, but an odd sort. A scent of sea and tar and strange spices."

Patch's eyes detected motion, and in the distance he saw brown legs.

"He's stopping often," Patch thought.

Patch crept to a dense part of the vines. He moved as if in the night now, summoning the stealth of his tribe, those ways passed on to each generation of raccoons and even improved upon in sacred confidentiality like the trade secrets of an artisan's guild. Patch came within one branch of the human. No longer needing his ears, he turned his eyes upward to ascertain this strange thing.

It was a boy, a manchild. He was eating mustang grapes.

CHAPTER 8

THE CHILD LEADS

THE boy turned toward the very branch where Patch was hiding, and the raccoon froze, knowing that he was still invisible and that to flee would only betray his presence. The manchild reached for a dark grape with his purple-stained fingers and plucked the fruit.

While the boy ate, Patch looked him in the face and forgot to be wary. Dried sand clung to the boy's cheeks and revealed tiny trails where water had run across them from his eyes. His mop of black hair, sculpted by drying brine, looked like ocean waves.

"Why does he seek food among these small wild grapes rather than inside an air-cooled manplace?" wondered Patch.

The boy pulled back the branch, plucked a grape from a dangling vine, and saw Patch looking right at him. Child and beast froze upon surprising one another. Patch came to his senses first but backed into a thick-branched guayacán tree, whose stubborn, woody arms blocked his escape. The boy, in turn, let go of the branch he had pulled back, and it whopped Patch on the nose. But the boy, too, was blocked after one step backward by a crowd of thorn-crested agave, whose needlepointed leaves held him hostage with delicate threats.

Something about the aroma of this particular manchild did not provoke the raccoon to flee. The boy's human odor was baptized in the sea—a strange mix of ocean and salt and spices, or *recado rojo* in the mantongue. There was an odor of tar as well, like stale diesel mixed with turpentine. Patch smelled a story still unfolding, one he needed to wait for and receive. It mixed with a memory that grew in Patch like a tender plant: a time when it was normal—more than that, eagerly expected—that a child would lead him. A memory that had yet to happen, yet had always been.

The boy remembered the grape between his thumb and forefinger. He looked at the vines and wondered. He pulled them back: there was Patch, who saw the grape. The raccoon's nose involuntarily quivered, pulling as it did on the recent memory of an incomplete lunch of that fruit at the cardinals' tree.

"Here you are," said the boy. "You may have it." He extended the grape to Patch.

What caused Patch to approach the hand and take the grape? He could never say. Even later in life, in his moonlit conversations with the owl named Salt under the ebony tree, he could never find the reason why he did it. Was it simple craving? No, for there were plenty of other mustang grapes to be had without the danger of Man, irritable cardinals notwithstanding. Was it charm? Had the boy somehow put the raccoon under a spell? Perhaps, but the boy's appearance was far from charming, except for his eyes, whose tears had washed them clean, cleaner than any other part of his body (for tears are meant to wash the inside, not the outside). And even if one could confidently assert that the boy had *enchanted* the raccoon, honesty compelled him to admit that the boy had not *intended* to charm him. The boy had just wanted to give him a grape. What is more, there was no discernable magic about the boy, only innocence—"a power greater by far," the owl commented. The only reason that held against any cross-examination was that Oracle had breathed on Patch, that Patch had remembered his true name, and that Patch had remembered Eden.

Patch savored the fruit, rather tart to humans, but to the animal tongue, good food. He was amazed at the lack of natural fear he felt, for normally Patch was on his guard in the presence of Man, lest a hunter or hound leap out and pursue him. But no one leaped out.

"I can give you more, if you'd like," said the boy. He gathered a few mustang grapes, a half dozen in all, and offered them. Patch decided to see what would happen if he took them, so he inched forward, stretched his neck out, and ate them from the palm of the boy's hand. The boy felt the raccoon's cold, moist nose and the gentle tickle of the whiskers. He felt the tongue searching his palm to ensure all food had been found. He was touching wildness, and it made him feel wild too.

Patch sat on his hindquarters and wondered. This boy seemed to come from a different tribe of Man than he had ever encountered. Patch reflected on the handful of six round grapes he had just received, and it reminded him of something. He darted around the guayacán tree and scurried off into the brush.

"Wait!" called the boy. "Come back!"

The sound of the raccoon running faded beyond the leaves. The boy scanned the wilds south and north of him, not sure which way to go. He sat bewildered for a while, but his thirst pushed him on, so he rose to look for water. At that moment, the return of the raccoon reached his ears. The boy heard the feet halt just short of emerging from the brush before him. He pulled back the branches, and there was Patch. He was holding out his paw, and in it was a marble. The boy blinked and widened his eyes.

The raccoon rolled the marble back and forth between his paws and held it out again.

"Your paws look like little hands!" the boy commented. "And, ooh, what a marble you have found!"

The boy admired the marble. Sunlight sprang off the curved surface. An ocean wave of color flowed within the gem, green touching blue and blue touching green. The boy gently grasped the marble, and as he did his hand brushed Patch's skin and claws. For a second the coolness and roundness of the stone and the warm aliveness of the little hand flowed through the boy's senses alongside one another like the wave within the marble, green touching blue and blue touching green.

The boy placed the marble in his pocket. It clicked against another one, a lone survivor from the bubbling sea where the boy had rescued it.

Afterward the boy searched for a pond and found one. Though it was green, he drank alongside the raccoon. Then the boy wandered into a wild orchard of tepeguaje trees and found a carpet of fallen moss and leaves. He played with the marble Patch had given him and the one he had rescued from the sea. Patch saw that two marbles were far too few to create an interesting game. From his hidden pouch in the hackberry tree, Patch brought a third marble to the boy's collection. The boy played. He grew sleepy. He curled up on his side on the moss and slept. Patch lay down for a rest too. Nose between his paws, he dozed off watching the boy.

* * *

From high above, Chalice watched them.

"I shall gather the flock," she said. Below her the tepeguaje trees gave way to the beach of El Realito, which in turn gave way to the Laguna Madre, the body of water between the South Texas mainland and South Padre Island. Red egrets and oystercatchers flew beneath her on errands of their own, but Chalice's thoughts were on one thing only. In the distance she saw a small island covered thick with trees: Green Island, a sanctuary Man had provided for thousands of birds. Chalice descended through the leafy canopy.

On the ground inside this secluded umbrella, Chalice lifted her head. There in a twisted, windswept cedar elm, whose branches all pointed toward the coast, sat Salt, a small, aging owl. He was rusty brown and decorated with patterns of gray feathers frosted with white. He was mediating a dispute. Before him two mockingbirds sought a ruling concerning the caracaras' attempt to build a new nest in a neighboring tall tree, an action that had infuriated the mockingbirds. They had laid their claim before Salt, protesting at length, often simultaneously and in the various voices of other birds, for a full hour. Salt had patiently listened. Only once did his head droop, and even then he caught himself in time so as to assume the pose of one deep in thought. After granting the mockingbirds serious consideration and acknowledging their "reminder" that they carried the honor of being the state bird of Texas, Salt had summoned the caracaras to argue in their own defense before the mockingbirds. But the latter would have none of it, considering it an insult to have to face the ones they were accusing, and they had flown off in indignation at the arrival of the caracaras.

"It appears your neighbors have granted you time to finish building your nest," Salt said. "Let us await their return after you have done so."

Salt heard Chalice call softly. He turned his head around—body still facing the caracaras—and he acknowledged her arrival with a polite nod. Turning back, Salt dismissed the caracaras, who bowed and bade him farewell.

"Greetings, Friend of the Northern Sky," Salt said.

"Hail to you, Bard with Golden Eyes," Chalice replied. "I greet you with peace."

"And you, Chalice."

"How are you?" the goose asked. "What is there to tell from your night flight over the mainland?"

"Only the same as I have told you before, I'm afraid," Salt lamented. "Clearing of land. Choking of roots."

"Yes," Chalice said. "It is as you say. Often, as I keep watch beneath the branches of the mainland trees in the heat of the day, I hear them whispering their sorrows to one another, groaning for relief. The trees of South Texas have much grief to bear."

"All creation groans, dear one," Salt replied, "and not just South Texas trees. The whole earth groans all day long. If only Man would listen. It may take a long time, but one day he will."

"I pray you will live long enough to see that," said Chalice.

"Thank you, kind one, but that is not for me to know," Salt replied. "However, be my remaining days short or long, I take comfort in the groan itself. For creation would not groan if it had no hope. It groans not only in the pain of death; creation groans for *re*-creation. This must mean that the new thing is still within the womb of what we have not yet seen. It means there is something alive yet to be born. Alive enough to bring pain, alive enough to bring hope."

Chalice made a nest out of these thoughts for a time. Then Salt spoke. "And what news have you, Chalice?"

"News of an unusual kind," the goose replied. "The pelicans informed me of an abandoned boy washed ashore. When I went to see for myself, I found he had survived. The sea had held him back from the realm of the dead below his waves. He had ferried the child to his brother the shore. The vultures were eager to break the law of plunder for the sake of his flesh, but I forbade it. The boy rose and wandered among the thickets of the mustang grapes, where he met a peculiar raccoon who befriended him. It all seemed so strange and marvelous that I knew I needed to summon the Colony of the Lost. With your permission, I will sound the call of the colony. I will show them the boy, for he—like us—is lost."

"You have permission," Salt said. And Chalice sounded the call. From beyond the branches came the reply of her flock, and one by one, each appeared.

A great blue heron, legs still dripping with water from the shoals, landed beside Chalice.

Next arrived a roseate spoonbill, his pink feathers tinged with the silt of brackish shallows. He bowed to the heron, picking up each spindly leg as if he were still wading through a marsh. The great blue tilted his straight spear of a beak and touched the spoonbill's rounded one in a greeting.

Then a whippoorwill announced her meek arrival from the branch of a hearty scrub oak above them.

Then came the sharp cry of an aplomado falcon, wings swishing the air as he found a branch thicker than the whippoorwill's.

And lastly, in a slow aerial circle whose shadow caused all to look up, came a neotropic cormorant with a fish in his mouth. He flapped his tattered wings for balance as his webbed feet, adapted for trees, chose a branch. Dried brine made his feathers stiff and ruffled. Through half-closed jaws he gave the call of his kind, a percolating cross between a coo and a cluck and a carpenter's drill. He swallowed his catch.

* * *

The seven winged ones turned in a silent cloud above the two sleepers like a mobile above an infant's crib. The Colony of the Lost landed in the trees and on the ground. They considered the sleeping boy. There were juice stains on his lips. His body rose and fell to the soft rhythm of his breathing and played a subtle melody that harmonized with the song of the wind above him. Nearby slept Patch.

"I conclude the child is a special one," Salt whispered. "By virtue of his immersion in the sea, he is not a normal Man, and by virtue of his unorthodox rescue, he is not destined for a normal path. And it is good the raccoon found him, for the sons of the House of Procyon are useful in tricky matters. They can make for a clever ending to a story, if not a happy one."

"Things such as this do not normally happen," said Chalice.

"Or perhaps," Salt commented, with golden eyes gazing, "such things normally happen, but we do not normally notice. This is why both the noticing and the thing we notice can be properly called a miracle."

Chalice watched these words fly a long, slow arc across her mind.

"Shall we call him 'Miracle,' then?" Chalice asked.

The owl turned his head around—body still facing the boy—and gave each bird an inquiring look.

"Yes," said the cormorant. "It fits like a fish in my beak."

"And a rock for my feet," said the heron.

"And the wind in my wings," said the falcon.

"And the moon in my song," said the whippoorwill.

"And the kiss of the sun when the day is done," said the spoonbill.

And so, in all the songs and poems the animals of South Texas made concerning the boy in the years that followed, he was known by that new name: Miracle. But the boy never knew.

The great blue heron spoke in a voice cracking with age. "Certainly Man will look for him, since he is a manchild."

"But for now he is lost," Chalice commented. "And the one Man who was with him abandoned him. It may be some time before the search for him begins."

"That makes him lost for some days, I reckon," said the spoonbill. "If he is lost, he is one of us for now, since we, too, are lost from our mates and our flocks."

"One of us—yes, one of us," said the whippoorwill in the clear three-note melody of her kind.

"And if he is one of us, then let us remain with him," said the falcon. "Let us make him an honorary member of the Colony of the Lost until he is found."

"Hear, hear," said the heron. "We shall take turns keeping watch over the boy until his elders find him."

"Shall we watch his friend too?" Chalice asked.

Salt looked at the sleeping raccoon. "Yes, his friend too," the owl replied.

"I shall go first," called the cormorant. "I have just had my fish, and I have strength to hold vigil while you friends feed. I will stay until the night watches have passed."

"Well done," Chalice rejoiced. "Well done, Swimmer with Wings. You use the strength the minnow gave you for a good purpose."

"But how shall the manchild feed?" the spoonbill asked.

"The palmettos will help him with their summer berries," the owl said, "and the honey mesquite trees have their sweet pods. The black persimmons are in the shady places. Let us hope hunger drives his feet to them."

And so, for the rest of the season that the boy was lost, the birds of the Colony of the Lost took turns watching him and his friend the raccoon.

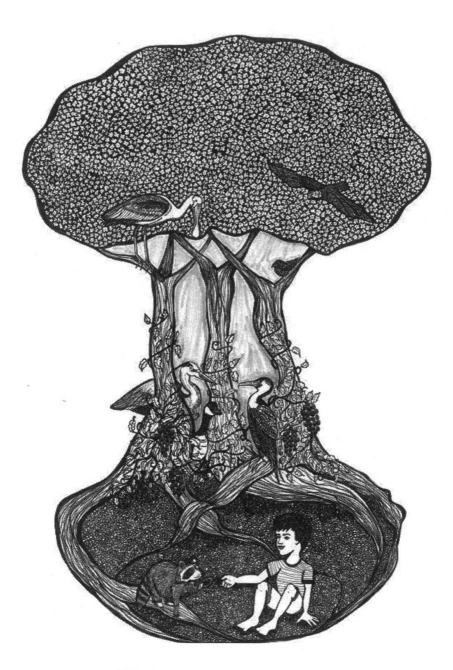

"Shall we call him 'Miracle,' then?"

CHAPTER 9

MIRACLE AND ORACLE

THE boy awakened from his afternoon nap and wandered into a field of yucca and clay mounds. Beyond these he saw an oak tree twisting its way toward the sky. Years ago wind had lopped off its upper trunk, such that the branches splayed outward rather than upward.

"The tree is waving to me to come," Miracle said. He went to the tree, and in her shade he found a bounty of black persimmons. Patch followed him into the shade and ate alongside him, standing on his hind legs to reach the persimmons while Miracle stood on tiptoe to reach the fruit that grew closest to the heart of the tree's outstretched arms.

The boy did not remain standing for long. Though the air was still, an ill-timed wind blew upon him. He felt light and heavy at the same time, as if his limbs were not quite there, and yet too thick to move. In the end, the heaviness prevailed, and he lay down. He felt as if he were bobbing up and down, though the solid ground, of course, was beneath him. But in his dreams, the soil became dark water, with currents warm and cold passing one after another over him, until the boy asked the dream to stop, and he became still and safe in his mother's arms. Night passed. Patch remained with him while the cormorant watched in silence from a tree.

"I must take him to Oracle in the morning," Patch said to himself, and he walked a slow circle about the boy until late in the night.

Thirst awakened the boy as the sun rose. He stood. A tingling weakness came over his legs and a sense of distress in his stomach, and these things, combined with the sorrow of his heart from what had happened in the sea, began to make him shake. He sat down. He pulled out his marbles.

"He still has too few," Patch thought. And he brought him a fourth from his hiding place in the hackberry tree.

As Miracle played with the marbles, the weakness of the boy's body retreated behind his curiosity about the game he played. He placed his face at eye level with the marbles. He watched the patterns they made as he sent one into the midst of the others. It was never the same pattern, yet always the faint rays of sunlight that passed through them kissed the ground from east to west.

The cormorant became hungry for another minnow meal and requested relief from the Colony of the Lost. The falcon volunteered to take the next turn of the watch. When he found the boy, it was clear even before he had landed that the manchild was in distress. The falcon descended and bowed to the raccoon.

"Greetings, Washer of Crabs," said the falcon, a bit aloof but still polite. "I am Sent of the High Air."

"Greetings, Bird of Far Sight," Patch replied. "So, the high air has sent you, eh? It must be important business you are on for a big wind to command it."

The falcon frowned. "You misunderstand me, wingless one," the falcon said. "My *name* is Sent, and my tribe hails from a place they call the High Air." The bird preened a wing and looked straight at the raccoon.

"Oh, I see!" Patch replied. "Pardon me! Well, anyway, greetings, Sent of the High Air. I am Patch of Palo Verde. A pleasure to meet you. See the boy I've found among the mustang grapes? He adores his treasures like my kind does."

"Yes, but I observe he is in need," replied Sent. "A subtle change is at work in him."

"You see more than I do," said Patch. "How did you come to watch him?"

"I am from the Colony of the Lost. We dwell on Green Island. Each of us has lost our mate, or flock, or both, and we now abide together, keeping watch for others who are lost. Chalice, the Canada goose of our flock, found the boy, and each member of our colony is taking turns watching him until he returns to his tribe."

Sent approached the boy, who looked up. The falcon bowed to him. ("For he is, after all, a child of Man, our ruler, and therefore a king," reasoned Sent to himself.) The boy stretched out his hand and touched the top of the bird's head. The smooth, gray-brown feathers felt as if they were from another world, one far above and free. Miracle did not keep his fingers on the raptor's head for long; he knew somehow that it was one thing to honor the falcon with a touch but quite another to stroke him as if he were a captive parakeet. The boy's hand quivered, and Sent felt it as he touched him.

"Yes," said Sent, "he is in need."

"I will take him to my new friend, the Lord of the Valley, and he will tell us what to do," said Patch.

"Your friend is the Lord of the Valley? There has never been one in all my days."

"Well, there's one now. A jaguar who prefers fish to fur found me yesterday. He let me help him after one of those nasty gars bit him."

"A jaguar?" asked Sent. "In the Valley? I have never seen one."

"Today, you shall see one!" said Patch with elation. "Come with me! We will take the boy to him together."

"The boy may be afraid," said the falcon. "When he sees the great cat, he may scream and run into the brush, where cacti and yucca will mock him with a scourging."

"But it may be worth a try," said Patch. "If the boy decides to be fascinated instead of frightened—and I would say that the chance of the one happening is exactly equal to the other—the Lord of the Valley may be able to guide him better than us. No coyote would dare harass him. I've heard of a coyote named Thud who does that to children, you know."

"A prudent thought," said Sent. "Let us take him to the jaguar and see what Miracle decides."

"Miracle?"

"So my flock has named him."

Patch touched the boy's back lightly with his paws as Miracle bent over to play marbles on his hands and knees. When Miracle looked up, he saw the raccoon walking away but looking back at him. The boy understood. He rose and followed.

Miracle reached a stand of willows where Patch waited. The low-hanging leaves hid from view who was behind them. Miracle lowered his head with a slight pout to the lips, unsure of what was happening but doing his best to be strong for it. Miracle chose to go through the curtain of the willow leaves.

Oracle received him with a calm purr.

The purr softened the boy's sudden dismay enough for him to remain steady before the beast. Oracle nodded to him and twitched the tip of his tail once. He bore neither teeth nor claws, for jaguars, like all cats, retract their claws when they do not need them. And the boy saw only the animal's calm and solemn face, mouth closed beneath soft, short fur that shone like gold velour. Oracle's demeanor was not dangerous, but it was not safe, either. It was the kind of comfort that does not pity you but gives you courage, should you want it.

The boy did not know what to do. His elders had told him terrifying tales about jaguars—how they ate everything: little children, big children, whole villages, even the moon itself! But the boy knew that to flee would be foolish. He could never outrun a mighty cat. He also knew it was useless to hit or kick the meat eater, for with one swipe of the jaguar's paw, he would become a slain and silent meal. But the purring penetrated the boy. It entered his mind and became a gentle channel into which, gradually, the flood of his fears poured, until his thoughts, one by one, streamed along like a gentle brook. The fear did not go away, but it did not rule him either. It now flowed in its proper place.

Patch entered the willow tree pavilion and stood beside the boy.

"Greetings, Fair Bandit," the jaguar said.

"Hello, Oracle," said Patch. "It's good to see you again."

"What gift have you brought me?"

"I've found a manchild alone in the wild," Patch said. "He was eating mustang grapes."

Sent stepped through the willow veil and joined them. "Hail, sire, Lord of the Valley," said the falcon as he bowed. "I am Sent of the High Air. The Colony of the Lost welcomes you to the realm of the Lady River."

"Greetings, Sent of the High Air," Oracle said. "Welcome to my lair."

"I have more of the tale, sire, if you are pleased to hear it," said the falcon.

"I am," said the Lord of the Valley. "Tell me your story."

"The sea brought the child to shore in the fourth watch of the night. The pelicans say that a Man was with him, but he abandoned the child, perhaps thinking him dead. Also, later that day, they saw pieces of a boat wandering about the waters of Laguna Madre looking for a dock. The boy is alone, it seems."

"We were puzzled about what to do," Patch explained, "for though he's a Man, he's still a child. And though he's from the rulers of our kingdom, he's not quite old enough to know his right paw from his left. We couldn't leave him alone, but we couldn't keep him without counsel either. So, we've brought the child to you, for you're the Lord of the Valley and will know what to do."

"How did you persuade the lad to follow you?"

"I sensed the boy might begin to worry, so I brought him a marble. He cooed like a dove and held it up to the light to peer inside of it, as if the marble were sharing a secret with him that it had never told me. He had another in his pocket. Then I brought him two more marbles…I think my other three would make his game complete. I can go get them, if you please."

"Well done, Patch," Oracle said. "You have befriended a manchild, a son of Man, our ruler. You have done so by letting him borrow your most precious treasures. You have lived by your own word: we are all borrowers of what we treasure, and it is good, therefore, to lend. Yes, in all this, you have done well."

Patch bowed. "Thank you, but I had not thought it through that much. To be honest, it just seemed the right thing to do, so I did it."

And the cat savored the raccoon's answer with amazement.

Oracle considered the boy Miracle, who stood admiring the cat. Then Miracle remembered how the falcon had let him touch his head. He tried the same with the jaguar. The cat obliged. The boy placed his hand on Oracle beside his right ear and scratched affectionately.

"What a good cat you are!" exclaimed the boy. "I must take you to Mamá and Papá so they can see you—if I can find them."

The boy's hand became still upon Oracle as his thoughts carried him to another place. He spoke aloud to a vision only he could see. "Oh, how dark it was!" he whispered. "How loud they shouted! I hope it didn't hurt. I hope they found the lighthouse."

The jaguar, the raccoon, and the falcon understood. They contemplated the boy's words: something dark and loud, something that might have hurt Mamá and Papá, and the lighthouse they were to go to. Every animal of the Valley knew of the lighthouse, for there was only one—a white tower of plaster-covered brick that had seen more than 160 springs. A light breeze blew, and through her the trees talked to one another in hushed voices about what they had just overheard. In the distance a chachalaca bird cried out his tribe's signature call, one that sounded like laughter to the human ear, though it was no laughing matter to the chachalaca. He was lost and searching for his kin. To the chachalaca, a laugh is a longing to be found.

The boy, shaking slightly, lay down a few steps away where the willow branches reached almost to the ground. He looked at Oracle until his eyelids grew heavy, rising and falling the way a small boat does when a wake of a greater ship passes beneath it. The three watched Miracle. His eyes slowly said farewell to them beneath a cloud of exhaustion and sorrow and curiosity. He slept.

"We need to take him to his parents," Oracle said. "We need to take him to the manplace he speaks of—the lighthouse."

"I know the place," Sent said. "Man also calls it *El Faro*. It is not far from here as I fly. For you, however, it is farther than a straight path, for many manplaces lie between here and there."

The sun went to work on the other side of the earth. The boy rose. He looked at the stars. The moon was rising in the south. "I will walk toward the moon," Miracle said. "Mamá was a friend of hers. The moon will know where she is." And he began to walk toward the lighthouse, though he did not know it. And the animals followed him.

The falcon escorted them above. His eyes became large to take in every trace of light the moon delighted to give. Periodically, he would descend and convey what he saw to Oracle as he and Patch made their way to the frontier between the wilds and the manplaces. There came a moment that Oracle and Patch stopped and looked in the direction Sent had counseled was best to go. Miracle noticed. He explored the way ahead and found a path through anacua and scrub oak trees that threaded its way between high fences and power lines. Miracle chose the path, and the animals followed.

At the edge of the wilds, they found a mound overlooking an irrigation ditch. From it Oracle surveyed long tracts of night-drenched farmland. Brush bordered each rectangular tract, creating zigzag patterns. Thrown at an oblique angle to the tracts and the brush was a convoluted series of resacas crawling away into the distance. Miracle silently signaled with a turn of his head, and they crossed into the farmland. The three traveled along the resacas, at times wading through them at their edges to avoid a fence. At the sight of the three night travelers, turtles dunked themselves into the dark water, but not before drinking in a good look. Small, silent bubbles revealed their whispered conversation in the murk below about what they had just seen. The three reached the border of a group of manplaces. The boy watched the falcon lean gently in the air to the left. Miracle turned left too. He led the jaguar and the raccoon around the manplaces through a field where grasshoppers sprang from blades of grass in every direction. The flurry of sound was so great that the travelers feared Man might awaken. But other than distant barking dogs, it seemed that no one stirred.

The travelers rejoined the chain of little lakes and followed their waters, hidden by both the sunken terrain and the thick growth at the waters' edge. The last bend was the most difficult one for Miracle, because he and the animals swam it to cross under a road that bridged it. They emerged to find themselves just beyond the manplaces at a refuge of yucca and mesquite and salty clay.

For the rest of the night, Miracle slept under a lone eucalyptus tree, while Oracle explored the way ahead. Patch went on what his tribe called a Borrow. He found a nearby manplace with its garage door open. The aging Frigidaire inside looked promising, so Patch opened it by holding the lower corner of the door and jerking his weight back. He returned with half a grapefruit and a chunk of cheddar cheese. However, knowing that the boy was thirsty, Patch hurried off on another Borrow to a home where he found access, thanks to the pet flap for the house poodle named Zha-Zha. Bribing the poodle with a juicy Rio Grande chirping frog—knocked out to stop its chirp—Patch returned with a can of Coca-Cola. He rolled it with his nose up to the cheek of the sleeping boy. It clacked against the circle of four marbles Miracle had arranged beside himself. Patch mused about the marbles.

"Still too few," he said.

With Oracle's permission, Patch journeyed back to the hackberry tree. In the sleeping hour just before dawn, he returned with his pouch. He fished out the remaining three marbles and dropped them beside the others, who clicked a gentle welcome to their friends. Then the raccoon hid the pouch in a hollow of the eucalyptus where a great root sank into the ground.

The sun rose and dried the travelers. They walked through the wilderness, and the heat soon compelled a rest under a stand of mesquite. Miracle ate a late breakfast—a manmade concoction known as Wonder Bread, which Patch had discretely lifted from an open box in the back of an unattended truck. Its preservatives had done their job of keeping the slices edible, and its additives gave Miracle the nutrition his morning Coca-Cola had lacked.

But by now Miracle had become very ill. The dark event that had engulfed the boy the night before Chalice had found him was seeping deeper into him. By midmorning a cough throttled his throat. Soon it became a rope clogging his lungs. By noon he could not stop coughing. Then dysentery answered the troubles Miracle knew had been at war within his gut since the time he had drunk from the green pond. He had to relieve himself often, each time becoming more dehydrated. His head began to burn, while goose bumps rose on his arms. Finally, too dizzy to remember his name, he lay on his back and stared at the concerned mesquite branches above him.

"I advise the healing herbs," counseled Oracle. The cat lifted his eyes to the mesquite trees.

"Greetings, You Who Know," he said to them. "Can you tell my companion the way to the healers?"

"Yes," the mesquite trees responded in whispered unison, "they are not far. If the Winged One will follow the dry creek bed toward the sea, he shall find them near the round stones, whom the healers comfort until the water comes."

"I am grateful," replied Oracle.

Sent nodded adieu to the cat and flew off. Oracle turned to Patch.

"What does the House of Procyon know of medicine?" he asked.

"Oh, as much as the aplomado, perhaps even more!" replied Patch.

"Go and gather what you know," said Oracle. "I will keep watch over the child."

Patch bowed and departed.

Oracle stretched out alongside Miracle, who lingered somewhere between sleep and delirium. He felt the fur of the animal on his skin, and its warm-blooded aliveness began to flow into him like a calmly rising tide. Miracle knew it was the jaguar, but the fever and fatigue had befriended him enough to take his fears completely out of reach. So, he lay there and let the warmth of the jaguar cover him.

Sent returned with the leaves of the Mexican olive tree in his beak, leaves called *anacahuita* in the Spanish tongue. And in Sent's talons were the twigs of the amargoso plant.

"The leaves are for his breath, and the twigs are for his bowels," the falcon told Oracle. "But the amargoso told me I must boil the mixture in water, and this is a thing Man must do."

Sent laid the leaves and twigs beside Miracle's left side while Oracle remained lying on his right. The falcon flew off to gather more herbs.

Then Patch returned with early tasajillo berries of the desert Christmas cactus. The berries were more green than pink and far from the bright red they would become in winter, when their healing virtue would reach its ripest. Patch placed the berries beside the twigs and leaves and inspected the sleeping Miracle with worried sniffs to his face. The boy stirred slightly in response to the cold nose and whiskers. He coughed but did not open his eyes.

"Ah, he's alive," Patch said. "That's good."

"If he were dead, would I not have told you?" Oracle purred.

"Pardon me, sire, but I was so concerned about the manchild that I forgot to ask you," the raccoon said.

"Forgetting me but remembering the child is the same thing as remembering me, since I too am concerned for him," said Oracle. And he looked toward the place where he sensed the imminent arrival of the falcon, who at that moment dropped through the mesquite and landed beside him.

"Here are more healers," Sent said, "but who will boil them?"

Patch cocked his head and squinted at the leaves and twigs until he heard what they were saying.

"I have an idea!" he said and dashed into the brush.

CHAPTER 10

SUN TEA

PATCH returned with an empty Dr Pepper can caked with a clod of dried mud. After tapping the clod off the can, he began to wrestle with it using his teeth and claws.

Oracle watched calmly, but the falcon was perturbed.

"Patch," he asked, "what are you doing playing with that mancan? Is *that* your idea—to play while the boy suffers?"

"Not play..." Patch said through clenched teeth, so it sounded like "thlay." Then he added, "No, not that...helth! Helth!"

"Do you mean *help* or *health*?" Sent asked, a bit put out that he, a falcon, had to ask such a question to a raccoon.

Patch stopped wrestling the Dr Pepper can and spit dust off his tongue.

"No, sir," said Patch, "I mean *both*. 'Help'...'health'...take it either way or both ways! Sometimes a raccoon can talk better with something between his teeth!"

Oracle looked away to hide his grin, knowing that Sent might take it as making sport of him.

Patch continued, "When Man camps, he uses these shiny buckets—see. Most of the time, they use wood fire or the blue flame from the secret places beneath the sand, but sometimes they use the *sun* to heat their water!" Patch held up the can, now somewhat crumpled from their wrestling match. "They catch the sun's rays inside, and the rays make the water upset enough to become hot before it kicks the rays back out!" Patch held the can above his head and rose on his haunches for joy.

"You describe it well," commented Sent. He lifted his head with the air of annoyance that occurs from a superior idea in the presence of the unlearned. "However, you miss one important detail: you are destroying the can, not opening it to its ray catchers. Allow me to help you."

Patch realized he had become carried away with himself, and he meekly lowered the beat-up can to the ground. Then he set himself on all fours and backed away from it, bowing to the falcon as he did.

Sent stepped forward and eyed the can as a bird of prey eyes a crippled mouse. (The can, on his part, knew that this was the end, but he kept a stiff upper lip against his fears and therefore caught a glimpse of glory.) The falcon grasped it with one claw and tore into it with the other. Moving his head back and forth, Sent used the hard point of his beak to tear the aluminum cylinder asunder. Then he set the bottom portion before Patch.

"Here you are," he said with a tone of gratulation at having done it. "I have provided the *help*; now *you* provide the *health*. Do what you know to do."

Patch carried the can to a resaca, dipped it in the clearest part he could find, and returned. He set the water in the blaze of the midday sun. Then he chewed apart each healing leaf and twig with his teeth and tossed them into the water.

The mixture became hot, but it did not boil. Patch frowned.

Oracle looked at Sent and knew it was time. He spoke. "Sent of the High Air, you have done well. But I have something that will help you do better. It is something you have forgotten. Let me help you remember it."

The falcon saw that the words, though simple, were the surface of a very deep lake—a lake that held both the reflection of the sky and the mysteries of life below. He bowed before the jaguar.

Oracle breathed on Sent. Suddenly the falcon was moving on a current of air that was from neither the gulf nor the earth. He was perfectly still. The wind carried him to a story that unfolded its broad wings in his heart and mind—a story he had forgotten, though he had not realized he had ever known it until he heard it again. It was the story of the first falcon of his kind.

* * *

There was a bird unique among the falcons of Eden—unique because most of his relatives were merely bluish gray or brown—but one falcon had a distinctive field of white on his breast. One morning he looked up from his branch on the ebony tree and marveled at the sun. Below he heard Adam marveling too. Adam mused:

What is the source of your brilliant rays?
What is the course of your lucent days?
What is the cause of your shining bright?
Is it fire? Or wave? Or ether light?

The falcon heard the question.

"I shall fly to the sun and ask for him," he said. And upward he flew.

The sun was so pleased by the falcon's intrepid visit that he kissed him in brotherly affection, and the flame of the kiss took root in his heart. By the time he returned to earth, his white breast had become red.

The peregrine falcon, who was the fastest of the birds, scolded him when he learned of the deed. "How could you do such an impetuous thing as to try to fly to the sun? Didn't you know that the sun is too far away, and even if you *could* reach him, he would devour you by his power? Why, whole planets would become cinders if they went too close! And you are little more than a feather: the smallest of the falcons!"

"No one told me it was impossible," the red-breasted raptor replied, "so I did it."

The giraffe, grazing among the tops of the trees, overheard the conversation and whispered it into Adam's ear. (For giraffes can only whisper.) When Adam heard the story, he laughed heartily. He named the falcon *aplomado* ("self-confident"), saying, "If all of us lived with the aplomb of this bird, we would each shine as bright as the sun!"

* * *

The wind brought the aplomado falcon named Sent back to the sunbaked earth beside the dying boy, and Sent remembered his true name. He decided to live in his story. Up he flew to confer with the sun. Higher and higher he ascended, a spiral ever narrower, until the air was so thin that it could lift him no longer. And yet he flew.

The sun, who loved the falcon, rejoiced to see him.

"Welcome, brave bird!" the sun said. "Welcome to my sky! I have made it rich for you! Updrafts and downdrafts! Rejoice with me! Soar and dive!"

"Thank you for your welcome," said Sent, "but I come with an urgent matter from down below. It is the matter of a boy far from his manplace. The sea has helped him, and now so have the animals, but the plants need your help to bring him back to health. He is very ill, so they have become a tea for him. Can you dip a ray into their brew below?"

The sun smiled in delight. "If the sea and the sons of the earth have helped him, then the champion of the sky should not remain asleep. I shall help, too! Show me the boy and the brew he must drink."

Sent wheeled with such a steep arc that it caused him to descend like a dart toward the mesquite trees. Down, down he flew. A cloud of dust rose in honor of his landing. Beside him was the cup and the worried Patch, wringing his paws. Sent looked at the sun.

"Here you are, friend," he called out. "Here is where I need you."

The sun gazed beatifically upon them. The falcon and the raccoon were not aware of any change of the light, but the hissing of water on hot metal caused them to turn simultaneously toward the cup. They could not see it, for it was covered in a steam cloud. The steam dissipated, and there beneath it was a dark cup of tea, its herbaceous aroma filling the noses of the bird and the bandit.

* * *

Miracle felt a wet, warm kiss over and over on his face. In a rhythm parallel to the beating of his heart—which, somehow, beat strongly as he awakened—the kissing continued. The tongue was rough as it drew itself across Miracle's face, but it was not a roughness like sandpaper. It recalled him to life, pulling just enough to stir him but not enough to hurt him.

The boy blinked his eyes open to behold the face of Oracle, with no more distance between the two of them than an eyelash. The jaguar was licking him. Miracle involuntarily sputtered the way a child does when his mother tries to wipe his mouth or nose. He propped himself up on his two elbows, whereupon the jaguar stopped.

Oracle looked toward the steaming tea. Miracle looked too. "For me?" he asked.

Oracle rose and moved a few feet beyond the other side of the cup, where he reclined and turned his eyes toward the boy.

Miracle crawled to the cup, lifted it by the rim with the tips of his fingers (for the metal was hot), and sipped.

Patch sat beside Miracle while he drank, pulling the spines off the tasajillo berries. Each time Patch finished removing the thorns from one, he handed it to Miracle, who chewed it between sips. The berry juice felt good in his throat; the cough faded away. He could breathe again.

Sent bowed to Oracle.

"I am grateful," the falcon said.

"I am glad," said the jaguar.

"By your leave, I would like to inform the oldest owl of the Valley of the events of these days. His name is Salt. He is the sage of the Colony of the Lost. He is rich in counsel and perhaps may prove useful to you as you meet the animals of the Valley."

"Very well," said Oracle. "Give him my greetings."

The falcon flew away.

Patch finished his work with the spines. It was time to go on another Borrow. He looked longingly at Miracle in silent farewell.

"He has my treasures," said Patch to himself. "They will keep him company, and he will keep them safe." And he departed.

Miracle chewed long on the last berry and emptied the cup. Then he pulled out the seven marbles and placed them in the dust before him. He looked at the seven until the sun withdrew behind the tops of the trees and almost touched the boy's feet with the light he cast through the glassy stones.

Oracle looked at Miracle.

"Tell me your story," he said.

The boy understood the jaguar, though no mouth moved and no sound was heard. He was not shocked. Perhaps he was too tired to be alarmed. Perhaps the tea had healed more than his body. Besides, if Miracle took it for granted that the jaguar had spoken to him, Oracle's request was no cause for offense. Children are that way. At any rate, no one ever asked the boy why he did not fear. And no one would have ever known about the conversation he had with the jaguar, had it not been for an aloe vera plant nearby who listened, took the words into her soothing heart, and stored there what was said. This is the story the boy told Oracle.

* * *

"My name is Francisco del Nombre, but Mamá and Papá call me Paco. I am from Mérida in the Yucatán. One day, Mamá and Papá told me we were going on a long journey. 'You can only take ten marbles,' they told me. So I took ten in a box and left all the rest with Tío and Tía in the village. They are in a jar. They promised to keep them safe.

"We climbed into a big metal box on the back of a truck. Mamá told me we would not come back to our house for a very long time. The ride was slow and bumpy, and that is how I learned what 'a very long time' means.

"'Where are we going?' I asked.

"'To San Antonio,' said Papá.

"'Is it as big as Mérida?' I asked.

"'Oh yes, and more,' he said.

"'Does it have *raspas* with cherry syrup?'

"'Oh yes, and more,' he said.

"One night the bumping stopped. Two other people joined us. They brought a quilt, and we all sat on it. I did not understand what they were saying. It sounded like Spanish, but the words were mixed with funny sounds. They smiled at me and asked me to teach them how to play marbles.

"One night all of us got out of the big metal box. Everything was quiet. We were near the water, and it smelled like fish. Mamá carried me. I said, 'I can walk, Mamá,' but she said, 'This time I have to carry you,' so she did. We went out onto a big, wooden bridge in the water that did not have land on the other side of it. A boat was there instead—a rusty boat with the paint coming off. It moved up and down. I bumped my head while Mamá climbed up the side, but

I did not cry, because Papá was very angry. 'Be quiet!' he said. He put his hand on my mouth. I had never seen Papá angry like that before.

"On the boat was a man named Tío Sergio. He was strange. He did not smile, and he wore sunglasses, even though it was night! How could he see in the dark? Anyway, Tío Sergio showed us some stairs that looked like the stairs to the slide of the playground at school. We climbed down them, and Tío made us crawl over a big pile of sacks full of gray sand. Papá found a door. It was very rusty. He pulled hard, and we went inside. It was dark and smelled like the place where Papá fixes cars.

"'We are in the United States,' Mamá said. 'You have to be brave and very quiet until it is time to get out at the lighthouse.'

"'OK,' I told her, and I went to sleep.

"But the boat woke me up because it was shouting at something that wanted to push her down. Then the water came into our room. We did not want it there. We tried to stop it, but it would not stop! We tried to open the door, but the pile of sacks did not want us to get out! We cried and cried and pushed and pushed. Mamá lifted me, Papá pushed me, and I went out a little hole. Then I was in the water with Tío, and he was angry. He grabbed me and gave me the orange thing to float. We swam, but the boat went away! It went away!"

* * *

Paco became silent, for the rest of the story was still happening to him, and he did not yet have the words to tell it. So his tears finished the tale for him. Paco sat with his knees folded to his face, clasping his arms about his shins. Each drop traveled down his skin in reluctant but inevitable tributaries along his legs.

Oracle rose and walked slowly to Paco with his head hung down. The Lord of the Valley bowed his head and licked the tears from the salty dust of the boy's feet.

Paco tells his story.

CHAPTER 11

THE ERRAND

THE next morning, Paco awakened with fresh hope and strength.

"I must find the lighthouse," he said, and he led his friends in the direction he thought it might be, the same direction the falcon above had guided them the night before.

The boy led them by way of thickets bordering fallow fields. All day, gusts of wind blew the trees in bending commotion above them. The wind was hot, and its touch inspired silence more than sound. But even without words, the three found that they traveled closer to one another than they had the day before. The hot wind drew them together.

At dusk Paco, Patch, and Oracle reached the waters of a grand resaca. They followed it as it made a great loop north and passed through a grassy gap between manplaces before it turned south. They crossed a culvert and peered through the pampas grass on the other side. They found themselves at the border of a ranch. A sign announced its name in letters so new they still gave off the smell of the paint buckets they had come from:

EDEN'S BEND
PRIVATE PROPERTY
KEEP OUT

Rustless ironthorn fences tied down the land. The cedar posts holding up the wires glistened with a bright coat of orange. Beyond the fence a windmill-driven water pump turned, though the manmade pond at its base—a place known in the local tongue as a "stock tank"—was very low on water, more a muddy crater than a pond. Cattle lowed from somewhere inside a mesquite thicket. A road white with freshly poured limestone gravel pushed its way through the savannah terrain. And in the distance, beyond a row of Washingtonia palms, was a small stable. It was not new. It was not painted. It leaned slightly, patched with fraying plywood and surviving planks from an extinct barn. The stable slept under a coat of rust on its corrugated sheet metal roof. The path to it was well worn. Beyond it was a thicket of ivy and thorns.

"Who lives there, I wonder?" asked Patch.

"Someone who was here before the road and the ironthorn," Oracle said.

A pickup truck roared by, its bed banging over bumps. The truck passed and disappeared at a bend where anacua trees bordered the road. Oracle hopped the fence, using the top of a post as a spring point for his paw. He jumped, flattened himself on the ground below, and sped across the road, flipping pebbles behind him as he ran. Oracle crept to the far end of the stock tank. Looking back, he saw Patch and Paco still carefully picking their way through the ironthorn. Patch had carefully laid his paws between the barbs and pulled a wire down, widening the space to help the boy pass through. But sticker burs ambushed the boy's bare feet. Once on the other side, he sat down, leaning on the fence post, and he began to carefully pull out the burs.

Patch joined Oracle. While they waited for the boy, they peered over the forward end of the stock tank, considering the occupied territory before them as if they were soldiers in a trench.

"Sorry we're so slow," Patch said. "I wish we could leap fences like you. Thanks for waiting for us."

"Waiting is good," Oracle said, still scanning the horizon, "for haste will put the lighthouse out of reach. But stealth is my concern, Patch. The closer to the lighthouse we get, the harder it will become to travel as a group of three. The roads are seldom empty. In some places the manmachines make a single, solid caravan covering the highway. The sight of our traveling band of eight legs plus two will make Man stop and perhaps surround us. Therefore, I think it is best that we become a smaller party."

"A good idea," Patch said. "You and the manchild will make a good pair. He can do the things that require hands, and you can do the things that require paws."

"No, Patch, *you* and the manchild make a good pair, for *you* have hands that are like paws, *and* paws that are like hands. You are just the companion the boy needs."

"What? Me? But sire, I—"

"You can make your way more freely than I can. If Man sees you, he may let you pass, but if Man sees me, he may not let me pass. For I am a jaguar. Too wild. Too free. This may place the boy in danger of never reaching the lighthouse."

"I see," said Patch.

"What is more, I have put my paw forward to find the Lonely Tree. I must continue my search. And I must meet the stewards of the Valley in a Council of the Cats."

"That would be Pace the ocelot and Force the bobcat you're needing to see if you're wanting the stewards," Patch said. "I mentioned them before once, that first night at Gar Pond."

"Yes," Oracle said, "a very old cypress tree told me the same on the night I crossed the Lady River. I must see the stewards. Then I must go with them to the Sanctuary of Sabal Palms to awaken what has slumbered since Kahoo fell asleep."

"I see how important it is for us to part ways so you can pick up where he left off," Patch said. "There hasn't been a Court of the Animals since my great-great-great-great grandfather Gus. But

I worry, Oracle. The boy is tired after the beating the wind gave us today. Tomorrow will bring him no strength, unless it rains, and it hasn't done that since the pink moon of spring. And what about the coyotes? And—oh—the dogs of Man! Such merciless beasts! I fear that Miracle won't reach the lighthouse without some help greater than I can come up with."

"That is where your raccoon ways come into play," Oracle said. "Did you not tell me that there is a secret skill for every band on your tail?" He purred as he looked at Patch.

"Well, um, yes, there is a secret for every ring. In fact, one of the secrets is that each ring holds five more secrets! That's the biggest secret right there—a way to get more out of each of our rings—but I'm not supposed to tell that part to anyone. Oh, me! I'm a mess! Oracle, I'm too small to defend the child! Please don't go. I've got skill, but you've got strength and size!"

"When skill is large, it matters not how small the body," Oracle said. And he let silence bathe the conversation and the raccoon.

Patch considered what the jaguar said. He noticed that the cat had more rings on his tail than his own.

"Well, with as many rings as you have," said Patch, "I don't suppose you could make a mistake telling me the things you've told me." He swallowed as if there were a cotton ball in his throat. He managed to get it down.

Oracle looked at Patch with patient, beryl-green eyes. It was not the fierce stare he had leveled at Ghast when the stubborn alligator threatened him eye to eye. It was contentment. It was admiration. It was taking pleasure in a friend with no thought to a limit of time. The raccoon found no coercion in the look, no sense of fear or fang. Only faith that all would be well.

"All right," Patch said, "I'll do my best to take the boy through the manplaces to the lighthouse. But what if his parents aren't there?"

"You will find out when you reach the lighthouse. Then you will decide what to do, if that is what you find. And you will know what to do, because you know who you are. You remember your name."

The words gave no clear picture, but they did give comfort. This seemed enough for Patch.

"I accept the errand, sire," he said. "I'm glad to help."

Paco joined Patch and Oracle, limping a bit from the ambush of the sticker burs. The three travelers walked to the palm trees. Beside them was a space of freshly cleared earth. The faded boards of an old house, stripped of every doorknob, latch, and hinge, lay stacked in a loose pile nearby. A path led away from the space and split in two directions—one going into the mesquite, another leading to the leaning stable.

Paco rested by the boards, rubbing his feet. A Gulf Coast toad began its evening song. The moon and the stars started to shine in the meekness of the sky of the first watch. Sent returned from his visit to Green Island, where Salt had learned of Oracle. The sound of the flapping of the falcon's wings in the crown of a palm tree caused Paco to look up. The falcon bowed to him. When Paco looked back down, he found that the jaguar and the raccoon were facing one another, almost touching nose to nose.

Oracle placed a gentle paw on Patch's head.

"Keep well," he said, "and remember your name."

"Yes, sire. It's been good to be with you. I hope we can fish together again some evening. I'm glad to be friends with a jaguar who prefers fish to fur."

Oracle turned to the boy Miracle and looked into his eyes for what seemed to be a whole season of moons—a length of time long enough for the boy to remember everything he knew about Mamá, Papá, his home in Mérida, his marbles both there and here, and his sorrow in the sea. Then Oracle bowed his head before him and waited. The boy knew his part. He placed his hand on the jaguar's head and blessed him.

"Good-bye, good cat," Paco said. "See you soon. The moon will watch us both. She has been watching all along."

The jaguar watched the raccoon and the boy depart. Sent bowed farewell to the Lord of the Valley and followed them in the air with a long, slow circle. Oracle saw them reach the well-worn path and follow it to the sleeping shed. As they grew smaller in the distance, Oracle's body began to speak to him of the need for food.

* * *

Oracle returned to the resaca that had led him to the border of Eden's Bend. He reached the northernmost portion, where it bent in a great loop with both ends of its oxbow shape turning southward. He reclined on the bank and watched the moon reflected in the water.

"Which way should I go?" he whispered to her. "North is the only clue I have, but this resaca points both its arms south. I have left my friend in charge of the boy to take him that way, for that is the direction toward the lighthouse. But where is the Lonely Tree? I do not know." And he paced the bank of the lake while the moon kept watch, listening. Hunger spoke to Oracle again with the strain of unwelcome longing.

Oracle crossed the resaca north. A barbed wire fence, brittle with rust, leaned and sank into the water in weak attempt at dividing the shore between one owner and another. Oracle stepped over the sagging lines. He reached a place where a tangled stand of oaks grew near the shore. Thick brush filled the small spaces between the low-hanging branches. Nearby on the bank, Oracle found a mound of earth heaped to an unnatural height in relation to the rest of the shore. Oracle stood upon it to view the resaca. He saw that Man had gouged out some of the pond bottom at the foot of the mound to build a dock that just cleared the water below it. A burned-out floodlight kept vain watch on a post at the end of the dock, the replacement of which had yet to make anyone's to-do list. A sign announced its presence, hanging on a rusted bolt at a tilt where the other bolt had fallen off:

BEAR CLAW RANCH
FISHING FORBIDDEN
OSO KENNEDY
OWNER

"I shall go fishing," Oracle said. He descended the mound to the dock. He reclined by the water, hovering his tail above it. After a while, largemouth bass began to appear at the surface, sleek and fat. Just as Oracle was about to slap one onto the dock, he heard an angry stomp.

"No fishing, trespasser!" snorted a voice from the trees. "Those are my master's bass and not yours! How dare you cross the mound of Bear Claw Ranch! How dare you live free of my master's command! Alien you are! Alien to here!"

Oracle saw two great horns rising out of the brush amid the oaks. Beneath them was a great, oblong head. Velvet ears drooped beneath the horns and framed a forehead as stern as an ancient pharaoh's. A brass nose ring drooped from his snout. Behind the horns, a hump the width of a human head raised itself atop a thick neck. With another stomp, the great body of the beast began to emerge: a Herford bull, a manbreed of the bovine tribes, a rival to the Brahman and the Angus in mass and size. Long did it take for the full length of his muscular frame to come out of the thicket. Dark and light splotches of various colors tattooed his hide and blurred into indistinct patterns. The bull ascended the mound and stared down at Oracle, the horns of the creature contrasting with the starry sky above them in a menacing silhouette. An odor of sweat and soil and high-grade feed crept along the earth to the surface of the dock where Oracle reclined. It pushed upon the cat's senses like the vanguard of an army.

Oracle wondered. "He speaks with no soul. How can this be? A tongue that moves but no heart behind it. Or is there?" He stood and extended his claws.

"I am a traveler from ten moons south of here, the jaguar Oracle by name. I come in answer to Kahoo the Grave, the last Lord of the Valley, who prayed from the Lonely Tree for a successor. The monarch butterfly told me the story, a tale from seventy springs ago. Here I am, the new Lord of the Valley and keeper of its waters."

The Hereford brandished his horns and lowed.

"I am the King of the Mound, 'Lord of the Valley,' whatever *that* is. I know nothing about what you speak. I am from the manplaces, created by him there and crowned king here. I am the sacred cow of his business. Without me, Man would have no cattle, no kingdom, no strength. For I *am* strength. He trusts in *me*. My horns are the gate to his hopes and my flesh his profit. So whatever 'lord' you are, it is under me. Under my hooves, under my horns." And the bull prepared to charge the jaguar below.

The Lord of the Valley considered the King of the Mound. He pondered the prospect before him, his tail lithe and twitching.

"This 'sacred cow' is not yet holy," he thought.

Then he spoke. "I warn you: there is a story that was here long before you were made, long before this mound of which you are king was ever dug up. It is the story that *is*. You had best hear it and walk its trail. Then your horns will have better foes to threaten than a cat going fishing."

The bull snorted and scraped the ground with a hoof.

"I do not know any story but my own, and that is the one I live in."

"Everyone's story adapts to the one before it, or it breaks away like fallen hail and melts and is no more."

"Prepare to fight, for I charge! On guard, Foe of Many Claws! Meet the Pride of the Master! Meet his hoofs and horns! On guard! I *charge*!"

And with that full warning, the King of the Mound hurtled down the slope at Oracle.

The cat had three choices. To receive the blow would have thrown him in the water wounded. To flee would leave him in the water still, though safe. But to be safe would be separation, and separation would not do. But to *run toward* the foe—that was a third way. Yes, for all its risk and folly, it *was* an option.

Oracle chose the third way. Up he leaped as the King of the Mound clomped upon the wooden dock. Oracle jumped between the points of the bull's horns, ran along his back, and sprang off his hindquarters onto the mound above. The King of the Mound turned and mounted a second charge. Oracle roared in warning, flattening his ears and backing away. He swung a threatening paw at the face of the bull, who flinched but threw his head and pinned Oracle's paw to the ground with the side of a horn. Oracle yanked it away with a cry as the bull lifted his hooves to pound him. The cat backed into the oak bramble, and both hooves came down in a storm of dust. Again the bull charged, this time scooping up Oracle with the end of his brass-ringed nose and throwing him against a gnarled oak trunk. In pain he slid to the ground as the bull charged again, but Oracle leaped upon a tangle of vines and branches that hung low beside him from the oak he had struck. The bull, in his haste and anger, continued to charge, heedless of the branches. The jaguar leaped away—but the head of the King of the Mound thrust through the midst of the branches. The bull tried to back out but could not! The branches and woody vines that crisscrossed the horns refused to give way. The bull pulled, but the branches clung to his horns, head, and ring of brass like spindled, aging fingers, too bent in some places to easily let go, too knobby in others—a wizened stubbornness that interwove with the untamed vines to fully arrest the bull.

In fear the King of the Mound threw his head at the closest branch, one thick but covered with conks of bracket fungus that had softened the wood. His horn gouged the branch and stuck there.

The Hereford struggled to free himself, but the more he did, the more the vines and branches held him. He stomped and struggled.

"Truce!" he cried out. "Troooce!" Then he stood still. Gradually his frantic breathing died down, and his heaving sides returned to a regular rhythm of rising and falling. Oracle watched from a distance until the foamy sweat of the bull ceased to slide down the bull's splotchy hide. Then Oracle drew near, limping from the pain in his forepaw. The bull looked at him with one wild eye.

"Come and kill me, Lord of the Valley!" he lowed. "Take away my shame! Such humiliation is not fit for the King of the Mound. Indecorous, I say! Indecorous! Rid me of this mockery! Pierce my head with your fangs and cut me away from this tangle! I shall die in honor before the King of the Beasts!"

"You shall not die," Oracle said, "at least not all of you. And I am not the King of the Beasts, only a Lord of the Valley."

"End my misery!"

"I think your misery lies somewhere other than where you think. You have relied on your horns, and they have gotten you into quite a tangle. Your greatest strength has proven to be your greatest weakness."

"If true, then treachery! I have betrayed myself!"

"I wouldn't call it betrayal. I would call it normal. For all share in common your condition: the greatest strength is also the greatest weakness. This is how it is for all living things this side of Eden. That is not humiliating, but it is humbling."

The bull heard the words, and for the first time in his engineered life, he listened. In the silence, a mourning dove sang from an alcove in the ancient oaks.

"Well then, if what you say is true, then please—if you please, Lord of the Valley—help me."

"Gladly."

Oracle hopped upon the thickest oak branch, wincing as he did from the pain the tree trunk had given him after the bull had tossed him into it. At first it seemed to the bull that the jaguar was about to attack him with treacherous intent to avenge the wound. But the cat remained on the branch and began to sway until the great old arm of the tree swayed too and with it the spindling arms of its choking strength. Moving back and forth and up and down, the jaguar caused the overtangled thicket to parallel his motion until the bull sensed an occasional looseness to the bramble he was lodged in. At the right moment, the mix of branch and vine opened, and the bull pulled his head out.

The King of the Mound stood next to the tree, eyes closed, thinking. Oracle made his way through the tree branches until he came to the one near the bull's head. Favoring the injured paw, Oracle leaned out and breathed upon the King of the Mound.

The Hereford felt as if something inside him was melting; even his title, "King of the Mound," now seemed to be of no more substance than a leaf floating on the surface of a pond. But in the depths of the pond, swimming like two schools of fish mixed together, was a story. The bull watched the fish in his mind's eye. He listened. And by the time the last fish had swum before his memory, the King of the Mound was no longer that. He was something much deeper—alive, in fact, for the first time. He had remembered his name.

CHAPTER 12

BOG AND PLOD

O N the floor of the forgotten stable of Eden's Bend, a Gulf
Coast toad sang a song to the accompaniment of a cricket
choir outside. His name was Bog, and he had chosen for
that night's performance "The Lay of Buford," a tried-and-true
tune from Louisiana about a renowned, wart-covered ancestor. His
listener was a retired workhorse named Plod. Plod was a seal-brown
bay with a sooty color bordering his eyes and nose and hooves. Here
is an excerpt from the two-hour, abridged version the old amphibian
sang that evening to his captive audience:

John Paul Jones in Bonhomme Richard
Serapis and cannon dared
Opened fire in sinking schooner
Took possession, prisoners spared

Like this ocean Hiawatha
Shunning white flag, shunning flight
Buford stood his ground and bellowed
"I've not yet begun to fight!

"Bring the barb and bring the javelin
Bring the trapper with his spear

Bring on Q-beam's blinding flashes
This old toad will never fear!

"You have come to bog a-sloshing
With your tools my hide to pierce
But I spring with legs galoshing
Coming at you bloating fierce!"

So next time you go a-roaming
Braving world beyond the pond
Wishing that in all these dangers
You possessed a magic wand

Wiping out the hunter's kingdom
Beak and bite and talon-claw
Overcome what stunts your wisdom
Face the terror, face the jaw!

Go down fighting! Give your best!
Croak your loudest in the test!
When the ghost you fin'lly yield
You shall make a tasty *meal!*

The horse was unmoved. He listened with half-closed eyes in that dream state that comes upon overstabled and underworked livestock. Apart from daily feedings and release to wander a weed-ridden pasture, nothing took place in the life of Plod except that slow fermentation process of the soul known to farmers and ranchers as becoming "barn sour."

Plod's ears rotated toward a noise at the stable door. Something was scratching at the latch of the smaller door set within it. When he heard the latch lift, Plod opened his eyes fully and turned his head away from the mildly offended Bog toward the noise of the inner door creaking open. Bog stoically concluded the thirty-ninth stanza of his ballad without an audience and leaned his squatty body in the direction Plod was facing.

Something trundled down the aisle of the stable toward them. Plod turned his body around and peered over the gate of his stall. A creature that looked like a small, waddling bear cub with a bushy, striped tail was approaching him.

"What do we have here?" Plod asked slowly, realizing the answer by the time he had finished the last syllable. "If you're looking for feed pellets, raccoon, you've come to the wrong place. All gone for now."

Bog raised himself on his sticky limbs. "And if you've come here for frog legs, you've come to the wrong place too!"

"You're a *toad*, not a frog," Plod corrected him.

"Of course I know I'm a toad," snapped back Bog. "I'm performing a diversionary tactic while holding on to my integrity. It is true, is it not, that there are no *frog* legs here?"

"Yes," Plod admitted in a low voice, "but I'm not sure there are any Buford kind of toads here either."

Bog took this personally and brooded in silence while his wound healed. Plod looked back over the stall gate, where Patch now greeted him with a polite bow.

"I'm Patch of Palo Verde. I've come from exploring Eden's Bend, where I have found that Man is busy building a new ranch out of old places patched together. I've not come here for horse feed or frog legs—or toad for that matter," explained Patch. "I've come for you, sir."

"Me?" asked Plod. "What do you need me for? I'm not fit to work; I'm retired. Can't you see my sagging back? I can neither pull nor carry a heavy load anymore."

"What great news!" Patch said.

"Great news?" asked Plod. "I just told you I *can't* pull and I *can't* carry the way I used to, and you're happy about it? Two thrown shoes don't make a gallop."

"It's great news because I'm not asking you to do what you used to do," replied Patch. "I'm asking you to do what you can do *now*. I have only a light load for you to carry, not a heavy one. It will be as easy as carrying your own full stomach after feeding time. You can still stand after you eat, can't you?"

"Yes."

"Well then," Patch reasoned, "you can certainly still stand with the load I'm asking you to place on your back! You'll barely notice it!"

"What 'load on my back'?" Plod asked with a neigh to the words. "Just because I *can* doesn't mean I *will*. What do you want me to carry for you?"

"I need you to carry a manchild to the lighthouse," Patch said.

Bog croaked.

"The lighthouse?" he shouted. "Preposterous! So far! So dangerous!"

Plod stomped his back hoof to silence the toad, who was less than one tongue strike away from the threatening mallet of the horse's foot.

"Why do you want me to do that?" asked Plod, dubious but intrigued by the prospect of relief from bleary-eyed boredom. "What would be important enough for me to leave my stable and my feed bucket for the lighthouse? I doubt I could reach it, and even if I did, my masters would only track me down. I'm not quite so invisible out here in the back forty acres that I could just trot off, you know."

"I know," Patch said, "but something has happened that makes it necessary to at least try."

"What has happened?" asked Plod.

Patch climbed the gate of the stall so he could look the horse in the eye, which was just beginning to cloud with a cataract.

"Something *new*," he said. Then he hesitated to say exactly what, for horses are deeply afraid of predators such as the jaguar, and nothing makes desire grow cold more quickly than fear.

"Something new?" scoffed Bog, who eyed the nearby hoof as he spoke. "Nothing ever changes here in the Valley. There's no room for 'something new.'"

"I don't agree with you, sir," insisted Patch, who decided that perhaps the news could be introduced more indirectly through a rhetorical chat with the toad. "Things are changing all the time in the Valley. Look at the machines Man uses, for example. They're bigger and swifter than the ones of the past."

"I don't call that change," Bog said. "Like horses before them…" He glanced up toward Plod, who gave him a look. "Yesterday's machines were prized and then forgotten. The day will come when today's prized machines will be forgotten too. Man will park them next to abandoned tractors, and together with the roof of the shed where the horse sleeps, the rust will claim them all. I do not call that change. I call that the same."

"Well, I see your point," said Patch, "but there are many other things that you can call 'change.'"

"Like what?" Bog challenged him.

"Well, for one thing, the deer realms bound by Coffee Port Road are now walled off with Man's ivy-covered brick. There was a time when deer gathered under the Mexican ash trees there in convention—with a coyote in the shadows to spy, of course—but now the deer must meet in secrecy for their counsel, places known only to the indigo snake."

"Why do you call *that* 'change'?" Bog argued. "Did not the *same* thing happen to the realms bound by Los Ebanos Avenue ten years before that? My uncle Albert, may he rest in peace, met a tire there. And before Los Ebanos was paved, did not the sabal palms of Lupe Farms give way to acres of grapefruit trees, causing the bat to rejoice and the squirrel to mourn? No, what you are telling me is the very *same* thing I have heard over and over again ever since I was a tadpole."

"It's the same but different," rebutted Patch. "It never happened on Coffee Port Road before. To Coffee Port, it's new."

"Coffee Port's story is the third verse of the same song," Bog insisted. "The deer have always been hemmed in by Man's trails. First there was a footpath, then two ruts for the wagon wheels, then an asphalt band—my uncle Edward, may he rest in peace, met a tire there. No, even for the deer realms, what is new is old; what is different is the same. Nothing new will ever happen here in the Valley."

In silence, each one pondered.

The horse swished his tail.

Patch thought.

"But Bog," he said, "why do we even have the word 'new' in the first place, if it will never happen?"

Bog said nothing.

Patch continued. "Certainly, if the word 'new' is in us, it's because there's hope that one day such will happen. I mean, certainly it's the seed of *something*. Certainly 'new' was indeed 'new' once—the very first time, before you and I were ever here. And if we still carry the word 'new,' it must certainly not have outlived its usefulness. Otherwise, the word would have faded away, forgotten in a wallow."

Plod idly muzzled his empty feed bucket, sending out a gentle backfire of pellet dust as he exhaled inside the container.

"Your words have flavor, Patch," the horse said as he blinked his eyes to clear them of the dust, "but I still have my doubts. I think folks just keep the word up in the same way Man keeps a kite flying. As long as he keeps hold of the string, the kite remains up. As long as we talk about 'new,' it stays alive. Cease talking about it, and 'new' will be no more."

Patch was not sure.

"But if 'new' was here before you and I ever were," the raccoon countered, "it would seem to me that 'new' will be here after you and I are not. I mean, this 'new' must be a thing outside of you and me, outside of our talking—not propped up by claws and paws, not propped up by anything at all. A thing that simply *is*, and therefore something new."

"You're just a raccoon, Patch, not a great horned owl!" Bog croaked. "You're a thief and a mischief maker! A crow with fur who likes shiny buttons and fishing lures! I would climb down from your tree of high-minded thinking if I were you. The further up you go, the more flimsy and swaying the tree. You may fall, or worse, be flung like a stone from a catapult. No, Patch, enough of your words. Come down to where the trunk is thick. Come down to solid ground."

Patch complied. He cleaned his forelegs and slowly bathed his face with tongue-wetted paws, bringing them down over and over from ears to nose, eyes closed, mouth in a frown. But he did not cease thinking.

"I agree with Bog," Plod said reluctantly. "We need to keep our feet under us, even if there is something new coming. I'm afraid that none of us can make something 'new' ever happen. And until it comes, we have to wait for it. We have to endure. We have to keep putting one hoof in front of the other. It's all we can do." And he sighed, his lips flapping that equine sound of surrender.

Everyone felt that the conversation had run its course. There was a collective sigh, and they felt closer in heart, if not in mind, after the argument. A cricket soloist played in responsive antiphony to the serenade of his brothers hidden in the grasses of the night. They played to moon and to meadow, to sleeping seeds and to watching stars. The friends listened. In the distance, an airplane hummed.

Behind his black bandit mask, Patch pondered what to do. Then he remembered his name. He excused himself and departed for the ranch-hand kitchen—the window, he had noticed, was propped open with a box fan that did not quite fill the space it had made.

* * *

Plod and Bog awoke to the sound of stones, so it seemed, dropping into the stall, followed by the gentle thump of four feet. Plod pushed himself up on his legs and shook off the straw, but not before Bog hopped upon his back in a surge of self-preservation from falling objects that compelled him to seize the high ground. The horse and the toad looked down and beheld Patch, beaming with pride, standing beside two bottles of lime-green Gatorade.

"I present to you a midnight snack," Patch said with a bow, whereupon he used his fingery paws to open a Gatorade. He held it up to Plod, whose nostrils flared in and out in a slow molecular analysis of the peculiar aroma of Man's mixture. The horse smelled the sugar and the salt, called "electrolytes" by Man, as a password for access to the inner circle of nutrition's mysteries. Plod's mouth watered. He gripped the bottle with it, raised his great head, and quaffed the entire contents.

A long whinny of electrolytic pleasure followed.

"Delicious," Plod whispered.

"Would you like another?" Patch asked, and he held up a new bottle. The sloshing, fluorescent contents cast Plod into a hypnotic trance as Patch unscrewed the top.

Inebriated with delight, Plod turned to Patch after dropping the second empty bottle. He looked at the raccoon with the spring-daisy gaze of a foal who has tasted mare's milk for the first time.

"There's more where that came from," Patch said, "and I can open each bottle for you. I am at your service with these paws of mine. All I ask is that you carry the light load I mentioned."

Plod considered, and, with the last of the lemon-lime still bursting on his tongue, it was a swift process to conclude what he should do.

"This is new," he said meekly. "Show me the light load."

Patch scampered to the door within the door and opened it. In stepped Paco.

The pleasure of the Gatorade dulled Plod's apprehension at seeing the lad, so he agreed to carry him.

"But you will need to place a halter on me," he instructed Patch, "or Man will consider me a loose horse, and we will not get very far on your journey."

Patch brought a rope lead to Plod, who worked together with the raccoon to place it on.

Paco watched with much amazement, but doubt dampened his wonder. He knew he had to mount the horse, and he even lifted the crossbar on the stable's double door in anticipation of the ride out. But when he stood next to Plod at the gate of his stall, the boy realized how immense the animal was. Patch sensed his hesitation, for Plod's size intimidated him too.

Patch looked about the stable. Draped over the gate of a neighboring stall was a deteriorating wool saddle blanket embroidered with designs. Thick threads hung loosely from its tattered end. Patch pulled them out with his teeth. They were dark gray and dusty white, the colors of indigo and persimmon, and the color of wine. Patch presented them to Paco, who clasped them gratefully and placed them in his pocket.

The boy set a foot upon the angled board of the stall gate. He reached up and grasped Plod's mane. Bog jumped to the floor. Paco swung his body over the horse and let his legs drop down each side. The toad, overlooking the indignity of the forced ejection from Plod's back, cleared his throat to gain an audience.

"Well, all things come to an end sooner or later," said Bog, "so I might as well go through the ending alongside you."

"What?" Plod asked. "You're coming too?"

"I may be small in stature, but so was Buford," he said, staring hard at Plod. "I will face the tires with you."

"Do you know the roads where you meet tires less often?" Patch eagerly asked. "It would seem in your tribe's interest to have learned them, and it would provide us with a better chance of reaching the lighthouse if you showed us that way."

"I know the Roads of the Rare Tire," he said, "and night is the best time to use them. But there are two harrowing passages nevertheless:

Peppervine Parkway—my uncle William met a tire there, may he rest in peace. And Southmost Road—poor Aunt Isabella, her legs were never the same after the Volkswagen Beetle she met. Have I ever told you about it?"

Plod cleared his throat. "Those are interesting tales, Bog, but let's hear them along the way. They'll make our travels go faster. Let the raccoon get us out of the ranch, and you can be the storyteller as well as the navigator from inside my mane."

"Yes," Patch agreed. "Let's not waste any time. Let's *hop to it* tonight!" They laughed as Plod lowered his head, and the toad made a cockpit for himself inside the black mane of the beast.

Paco knew he was hearing laughter; he laughed too.

Outside the stable, Patch raised himself on his hind legs and sniffed the air. Man? No. Coyotes? No. Dogs? One barked far away.

"What's the best way?" he asked.

"South," Bog replied. "Stick to this trail until we get to the sorghum field, then cross it to go east before turning south again.

"If we're going east, couldn't we just go behind the stable and cross that way?"

"That wouldn't work too well," Plod said. "There are vines out back thicker than kudzu and ivy put together. Thorns, too. Been that way since I was a foal. The old owner let it go, and the new owner is too busy to care about it yet."

"New owner?" asked Patch.

"The mockingbirds say his name is 'Tripp,' and they've taken up the habit of chirping it in their afternoon songs. They say he's pulling up the old fences and adding land to the place. By the time he's through, only King Ranch will be bigger, they boast."

"He must be building a very large manplace for himself."

"It's not that large, I'm told. The possums whisper that he's leaving most of the land for the animal kingdom. You can't trust everything a possum says, mind you, but I think there's something to it, because they're nervous when they speak about it—as if in telling the tale, someone might take it away. Now, let's get going. Leave the shortcut to the thorns. The old trail is better."

Patch led Plod and Paco down the trail until they reached the sorghum field. They crossed it. On the other side was a gate, which the raccoon opened with some difficulty. They moved through another sorghum plot in a relaxed manner as if nothing were wrong. For indeed, to move as if something were wrong might very well *make* something go wrong. Then they turned south.

Fog helped the band move undetected across the ranch. She had eavesdropped on Patch's persuasive speech in the stable, and she had agreed. Patch knew it, for he could see a slight variegation in the folds of her mist. She drew a soft swath of herself across the raccoon's shoulders, a milky movement, affirming, "You're on the right path, Patch. Keep going."

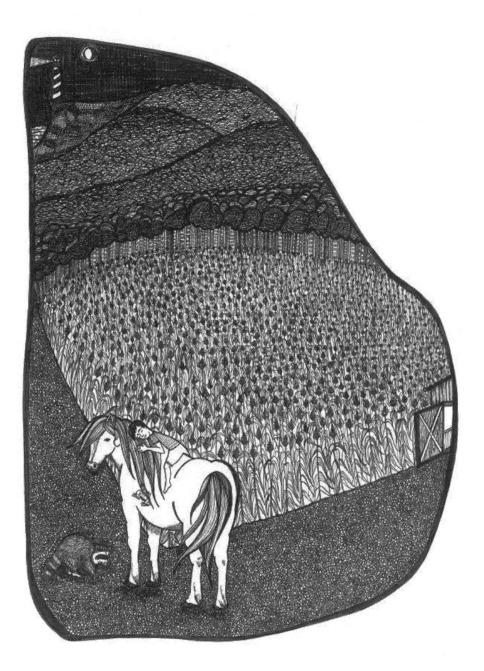

"You're on the right path, Patch. Keep going."

CHAPTER 13

BARBECUE ALLEY

THE four travelers passed the heat of the following day under a Mexican sycamore tree. Beside the sycamore was a broad quilting of cornfields, some strong and green from the diligence of farmers watering them, some tinged with the burned brown of drought, and others dried up altogether, standing like ghosts. But what they all had in common was that their height and their breadth created a gentle cover for the travelers to pass through. They rested several times among the stalks. Beyond these, a coop for free-range chickens also provided shade and a few morsels. From a farmhouse Patch retrieved food for Paco and a Gatorade for Plod. Bog feasted on flies too curious for their own good about the sweaty horse resting among the chickens. Then the party moved on until sunset.

Plod made his way down an unpaved road. Atop the horse, Paco lolled his head in near slumber. His body swayed as the horse's back gently rocked him. Bog dozed within Plod's mane, his sticky pads wrapped around clumps of coarse hair. Patch's feet were sore, but he thought it best to continue walking alongside Plod and not overtax the old horse with too heavy a burden. And though a boy on a horse in South Texas was not unusual enough to compel busy Man to stop, a raccoon on a horse would have complicated Man's priorities. So, for simplicity's sake, Patch walked.

Plod reached a paved, four-lane road with a broad, grassy esplanade in the middle. Manmachines drove by. Plod stopped.

"Where to now, Bog?" Plod asked.

"This road is like a river," the toad said. "There's no other way but to cross it. Wait till the moon has moved ahead of us, and the manmachines will be fewer."

The travelers waited while the moon moved ahead and the dusky sky darkened. Manmachines became fewer and fewer until eventually there were no headlights at all, from either end of the horizon. They crossed. Then, after walking through a forty-acre field, they came to an electric-light frontier of manplaces stretching across the black horizon—a vast manrealm called a suburb.

"This is where the going gets tough, comrades," Bog said. "There are no good ways around this thicket of manplaces. The only way through is the one in front of you. Nonetheless, it *is* night, and that can make it very much like the field we just crossed. Most of Man is asleep, and the ones who are awake are inside watching their black boxes."

"Black boxes?" Patch asked.

"Each one is like a pond," Bog explained. "Only it hangs sideways from the wall, and it reflects things. The shore of the pond is not green but black."

Patch thought. "Oh, yes!" he exclaimed. "I've seen them from around the corners of kitchens I've visited! They're noisy ponds, these sideways ones, and how the reflections wiggle and jump! So strange... Normally, when I see a reflection in a pond, I can look up and find the thing reflected, like a bird or tree or cloud. But those sideways ponds are different. I see the reflection, but when I look to where the reflected things should be, they aren't there—only empty space."

Patch led the way now, for he was familiar with how to find passages through suburbs.

"If you can get us to the other side of this manthicket," Bog said, "I know a weed-covered road that borders a ranch. If we can pass through it, we can reach the lighthouse."

"OK, I'll try," Patch said, but each manlight seemed to him a watchful eye against his hopes.

Most of the manplaces were fenced in, but Patch found a way between the backyards of two rows of them, a service alley for the power lines above and gas below. Patch led the travelers into this alley. A wall of wooden planks stood on each side of them. A grasshopper began to rattle his wings against his legs in a percussive chant.

"What's that all about?" Patch asked.

"Don't know," Bog said. "Maybe he's drunk on holly berries."

"It's not the time for grasshopper songs," Plod said. "I do believe he's talking to us, but I don't know the songs of the grasshoppers."

"I don't either," Bog said. "The Tribes of the Six Legs are reluctant to teach them to us. They don't see the point, I guess, when we might take in the singer along with his song."

The party continued, but more slowly, as Patch listened and sniffed the air every few steps. Then it found him: the nauseating smell of fresh canine droppings. There was no wind; dogs were nearby.

Patch did not need to analyze the odors much longer, for a sound grabbed his ears: the sniffing and snorting of noses pressed against a fence.

"Plod, do you sense where they are?" asked Patch.

"Yes, ahead on the right, my ears tell me," Plod whispered. "A few more steps and we'll break their boundary line. They'll bark to get free and tear us apart. Their master will come out, and we might get rounded up."

The travelers stood still.

"Maybe we should go back," Patch said. "I'll look for another grass alley between the manplaces."

"Go back? Retreat?" Bog said. "Never!"

"I didn't say 'retreat,' Bog. I said 'go back!'"

"It's the same thing!" Bog insisted. "Smells like yellow-bellied cowardice to me. I'm no tree frog that flinches; I'm a Gulf Coast toad who takes what comes to him, tires and all."

"Bog," Patch insisted, "it's *not* a retreat, and it's *not* yellow-bellied. It's…it's…advancing in a different direction!"

"Hmm, well, I never thought of it that way," Bog said.

"But there's no telling if another way will be any more clear of dogs than this one," Plod said. "I smell canines everywhere here."

A pickup truck appeared and parked in the street where they had come from.

"No use going back now," Plod said. "The Man in that car won't sit still and let us pass. He will try to corral us."

Patch saw the bright-orange dot of the Man's cigarette in the cab of the truck.

"Well," he concluded. "No way but forward, I guess."

"Onward and stalwart, come what may," chanted Bog, and he muttered the rest of the poem in a whisper like the rhythm of a drummer behind advancing infantry amid the ever-louder chants of the grasshoppers.

Ahead and on the right, two black muzzles protruded through holes that those same snouts had chewed open over the past month. Each nose lodged in a dirt rut it had made from jutting under the fence each time someone passed by. But this time, the muzzles found a faultline above them when they thrust themselves into the ruts: loose boards.

Plod deliberately let each hoof drop heavily to let the dogs know he was more than twice their size. The vibrations traveled through the earth to the bodies of the fenced predators, but in response came the unmistakable growl of a specific kind of Man's canine guards—a growl that was so full of strength that the very sound seemed to rip clothing apart. It was the warning call of the pit bull.

Patch hopped onto Plod, leaning on Paco's back, both for balance and to comfort the child. Paco heard the growling dogs too and felt a chill, though the night air was warm. The growls reminded him that his legs were bare and dangling.

Plod pulled on the days of his youth, when, as a feisty steed, he had reared above an angry cow dog and cowed him into submission. Plod's old body was not the same one it had been in that day, but the heart that had lain dormant had never been evicted. He awakened cow-dog courage and proceeded forward.

Growls turned to barks. Snarls pushed their way through foamy mouths. The travelers drew closer, and the anger of the pit bulls made the wood seem as thin as crepe paper.

The travelers were right next to them now. The barks seemed to come from lungs twice the size of their canine bodies, as if dragons were pumping bellowed air into them.

"I can't make sense of their speech," Patch said. "They've torn their words into pieces and thrown them about. I...I can't put them together."

The pit bulls shouted with such spit-filled hate that the ground underneath them was as raw meat they had slashed open.

"Steady, Plod, steady," said Bog, who clung tightly to the horse's mane and buried himself to its roots. His whispered cadence became wordless breaths.

Then it happened. The fence cracked open—first one chunk and then another—to reveal two black demon faces with white fangs, red tongues, and eyes darkened in the flame of rage.

Plod jolted instinctively away from the sudden burst of wooden shrapnel, and when he did, Paco lost his balance and fell on the ground before the pit bulls. Patch grabbed onto Plod's tail as he dropped, staring in terror at the shaking fence. Filled with bloodlust, the dogs now rammed their shoulders full force into the battered wood, their heads stretching out into the alleyway like a pair of gargoyles that had come alive.

Plod, who had jumped ahead, remembered Paco and overcame his impulse to flee. He turned around and stomped and whinnied at the dogs. One turned his maddened, frothy head toward Plod, but the other strained against the crumbling wood to lunge at Paco, whose two legs had failed him. Fear made him wobble with dizziness. He could not stand. He could not run.

Patch slid off Plod's tail and hit the ground running toward Paco. He stood between the shaking lad and the devil dogs, before whom Patch bore the teeth and claws of a raccoon defending his den.

Patch's intervention produced no more than a slight pause in the fury of the pit bulls as they adjusted their eyes to the presence of a second intruder. But Patch still met his goal. The pit bulls chose to focus their wrath on the closer prey—the furry one—while the hairless manchild struggled to his feet and stumbled toward Plod. The horse, sensing Paco's attempt to remount, backed up to the fence opposite the dogs. The boy's bare foot found a splinter-filled fence plank to push from, and Paco flung himself upon Plod's back. The horse fled.

A pit bull glowered at Patch with primal passion and charged. The fence gave way, and the raccoon found himself rolling under seventy pounds of attack dog. Patch fell backward. The dog's jaws snapped, and slimy teeth smashed against Patch's nose.

The raccoon called on a ring from his tail. The secret skill in it came alive.

Patch darted from under the pit bull while the dog's momentum continued to move him forward. Patch bolted for the hole in the fence and plunged straight into the backyard of the dogs. The pit bull outside the fence wheeled around to go after him, and the other pit bull, still straining to burst through the hole he was making, wriggled backward and turned. By the time the dogs were hurling themselves at Patch, he had reached the porch of the dogs' manplace. Above him were cedar beams with spaces for sky and clematis vines. He went up a supporting post, jumping onto a hanging plant on his way to the top. The pot swung as he leaped off. It careened back with the force of Patch's leap and unhooked itself, dropping on the head of one pit bull, who howled and scurried to the grass from the stun of the blow.

A light went on in a bedroom window of the manplace.

Patch saw both dogs look toward the hole, and he realized they had not forgotten Paco and Plod. Patch ran back and forth along the cedar beams. The scampering patter of his feet hooked the full attention of the pit bulls, whose instinct commanded hot pursuit of the closer, fast-moving prey. The dogs chased Patch from below, running along beneath him and barking fierce threats.

Through a gap in the beams, Patch saw a large gas grill on the porch, open with a tool lying in it, as if the owner had been cleaning it during the day. Next to the grill, on the brick wall of the house, was a cabinet. Patch had seen this setup before. He knew about grills, and he knew about cabinets next to them.

With a shout he dropped to the top of the cabinet. He jeered at the pit bulls, who, in blind rage, rose on their hind legs and placed their forepaws on the open grill. Patch jumped from the cabinet onto the heavy, half-barrel lid, which came slamming down on the paws of the dogs. They yelped in shock and wrenched their paws out.

Another light came on from somewhere inside the house, illuminating the glass of the sliding door to the porch.

Patch stretched a paw down and opened the cabinet. Inside were grilling utensils and containers of sauces and marinades Man always had on hand near his grills. He curled his body and dropped into the cabinet. While the dogs limped in circles, recovering from pain, Patch tossed one bottle after another onto the porch. Most were plastic and bounced; a few were glass and broke.

The pit bulls, angry and humiliated by the raccoon, were poised to leap and pull him down. But as they prepared to strike, a vast army of savory smells invaded their nostrils, aromas of barbecue, Worcestershire, ketchup, and salsa. The pit bulls found themselves completely surrounded, and so, after looking at one another, they surrendered to the smells without a fight. Hobbling about between pieces of broken glass and the spewed contents of squirt bottles, the pit bulls sniffed each sauce. At first they gingerly licked spilled samples, being careful not to cut themselves and sneezing when they came across cayenne pepper or jalapeños. But eventually each dog found a puddle of some delicacy and began to devour it as if he had not eaten for days.

Patch hopped from the porch cover to the roof of the manplace and from the manplace to the fence beside it. Quietly he moved along its top until he reached the grass alley. As the sliding door of the manplace porch opened, he dropped out of sight. The Man found two guilty-looking dogs in a mess of sauce and bottles.

By dawn, Patch caught up with the others on the weed-covered road. The grasshoppers gave him a four-winged ovation, for they had heard he was coming.

* * *

Oracle kept moving north, slower now as his body recovered from the hurts of the Hereford. But no plant or bird or creeping thing he met knew anything about the Lonely Tree. The land became broader, sandier. The dying ponds held undrinkable bracken and a kind of crawfish that spoke a language Oracle did not understand. Here and there a low dune hosted rugged, drought-hardened grasses. A stand of dwarf cedars created a welcome place of rest and shade. There he found an ironwork of Man, forgotten and covered with rust, where a family of horned lizards had made a den. There was a small furnace of some kind, a bucket, and rods covered with brittle vines that had perished long ago. And lying on the ground beside a decimated shell of a water trough was a branding iron, on which Oracle found a curious symbol:

Further on Oracle found a cottonwood tree—out of place it seemed, testifying to a time when the land had once been a well-watered place of marshes and reeds. The tree held on, but he was too weary to speak to Oracle without the help of the wind of the sea, who saw and gave the cottonwood the strength to sing through his gently clapping leaves:

I linger here
From year to year
Recall the past
For I am last.

Forgotten days
Of better ways
When lily ponds
Met sunrise dawns

In merry wood
Of creatures good
Where birds did sing
And Man was king.

Oracle tasted the sorrow and honored it with silence until the sun had set and the evening star appeared. Then he spoke to the cottonwood.

"Can you tell me the way to the Lonely Tree?" he asked. "I have heard her story, and I have come to live in it."

"I do not know the Lonely Tree," he whispered. "I myself am alone."

The jaguar thanked him. He marked the withered bark with the sign of his paw, and the cottonwood remembered the days when cats and many other things of fur and feather had gathered beneath and among his branches.

"Thank you," he whispered, and he returned to his sleep.

The jaguar continued north slowly, watching and listening to every breeze and blade of grass and footprint of the small creatures who dwelled there. Ascending a gentle dune, Oracle reclined, hidden by a stand of blackbrush and the spine-tipped leaves of a yucca plant—what Man calls Spanish dagger. From the dune he surveyed the land north of him: mesquite and prairie with sandy lowlands interspersed between. From the east the smell of the unseen sea reached him.

"All I know is to go north," he said to himself, "but the resacas no longer lead me that way. And this realm becomes less and less a realm of trees and more a meeting place of sand and scrub. It leads away from the Valley."

Oracle decided to wait. In the night he remained awake but did not move forward. The moon watched his waiting. Then, in the fourth watch of the night, quail hidden in the mesquite sang. Oracle listened, and so did the moon. This is what the hidden quail sang:

We face the south
Where lies the mouth
Of Lady River great and long

We turn around
We hear the sound
Of laughing waters in a song

We love the tree
The Lonely Tree
Where our forefathers said good-bye

To Kahoo brave
Kahoo the Grave
The night he prayed, the night he died.

CHAPTER 14

FROM THE CORNER
OF THE EYE

TO the south of Oracle, the travelers reached the border of the ranch Bog had told them about. That day they rested beside an abandoned manmachine and rusting household appliances, where uncut growth screened them from the road they had traveled. Warm air hung like thick curtains, and only now and then did the breezeless sky give a whisper of itself from the sea. Night fell, and Patch set out to scout the ranch for food and a way through. Plod dozed contentedly after downing three Gatorades Patch delivered to him, bottles the raccoon had borrowed from a lunch cooler in a farmer's toolshed. It took the raccoon three Borrows to bring them. After a fourth and fifth Borrow, Patch presented Paco with two snack bars from a sleeping RV with Michigan plates. And all the while, Bog sat on an old, wireless fencepost crooning an ode to his late uncle Albert, a slow but steady melody that calmed his companions into quiet, if not drowsy, contemplation.

Patch returned again.

Clunk.

Plod started at the sound. Bog cut his ode short at the forty-ninth stanza. Paco looked at his three companions as he opened the second snack bar.

Before Patch on the ground was a webcam.

"I got this from the open space we have to cross to get to the lighthouse," Patch said with confident delight. "The mice told me this manrealm is called Gaston Ranch. They called these things watchers and told me they were easy to chew through, and they were right. I chewed through one in no time. But I told them I could do even better than that; I could *untie* one. And look here—I did it! These machines are like eyes, you see. That's why they call them watchers. And without these eyes, Man won't see us. We can cross the whole manplace undetected!"

"What about the firestring?" asked Bog. "This ranch puts fire in the fences to keep their big-hoofed beasts from wandering off. See that line beside the ironthorn? The one with the glassy knobs? There's enough fire in that wire to make a toad jump to kingdom come!"

"The fireflies showed me it's turned off," said Patch. "They sat on it and flashed me cheerful signals that it's just a thornless ironwire with no fire at all. I touched it, and it didn't burn me."

"Why would Man leave it turned off?" asked Bog.

"I don't know," said Patch. "Maybe the owner of the manplace forgot."

"Sometimes they turn the firestring off when they drive their livestock away," Plod said. "In fact, I don't see any cattle—though I sure smell what they left behind."

Paco knew it was time to go. With the help of a juniper branch, he hoisted himself over Plod's back using his good foot—the one without splinters from the fence he had pushed upon to mount Plod in the alley with the pit bulls. For a moment, Paco lay crosswise on the horse's back like a saddle blanket, lingering that way because all the weight of his fears seemed to drop off on both sides of the animal through his hands and feet. Then he turned upon his stomach until the bristles of Plod's mane filled his face, and he sat up. Plod bowed his head toward the fencepost for Bog to hop on, and Patch led the way through the ranch he had just put to sleep.

* * *

The ranch hand thought he heard a high-pitched sound coming from somewhere inside ESPN. At first Burt thought it was an air horn from some face-painted fanatic in the televised crowd, but no, the noise was still there at the beer commercial. He got up, put the TV on mute, and tried to find the noise. When he opened the kitchen's walk-in pantry, the cooped-up blare of the alarm came rushing out, shoving him aside in its haste to leave. A red light burned brightly on the control panel of the ranch security system.

"Mel, take a look here," Burt said over his shoulder.

Another ranch hand came in.

"Yep?"

"Somebody's done yanked the 'lectric eye off. A vandal, I reckon. Better go check."

Burt glanced at the desktop computer as he walked to the gun cabinet. He saw a large, red pop-up: WEBCAM OFFLINE.

"Huh? That too? What the..."

Burt grabbed a semi-automatic AR-15 along with a lever-action Winchester rifle.

"Mel, call the house and wake the Man up. Could be trouble."

Mel looked at Burt's choice of weapons, one in each hand.

"You bringin' your army toy too?"

"Just in case it's somethin' serious," Burt said. "I like havin' plenty of backup." And he tossed the Winchester to Mel.

* * *

Patch led the travelers to the open space they had to cross. Before them was the long rectangle of a field upon which bales of machine-rolled hay awaited the day Mel and Burt would put them to work. The travelers entered the field. The hay bales, though silent, seemed to be sharing secrets with one another in a way that made Patch and his animal company feel rather uncomfortable.

A truck engine started in the distance. The animals looked. A pair of headlights broke the dark on the horizon.

"Didn't you put the ranch to sleep?" Bog asked.

"Yes, but a manmachine is different," Patch said, a bit defensively. He watched the pair of headlights move on a distant, two-rut lane. "It's a lot harder to put moving metal boxes to sleep. The wire I untied doesn't reach inside those."

The far headlights slowed to a stop. The travelers saw shadows cross in front of the lights. Then, moving away from the truck, two floating, luminous globes probed the dark. One darted here and there in quick glances at each bush. The other peered methodically across a field of cut grass.

"Patch," Plod said, "I think someone knows we're here."

"We might want to turn around," Patch replied.

"Turn?" asked Bog. "And have them spear us in our backs? No, let us meet them with our eyes in *front*!"

"Let's put our eyes behind a haystack first," Plod advised, and the travelers moved to the closest one between them and the distant flashlights.

From his vantage point on the horse, Paco watched the search beams moving silently on the horizon. Their path was oblique in relation to him and his friends; he saw them become smaller and then disappear. The boy relaxed and looked around at the hayfield.

The barrel-shaped bales of hay lay equidistant from one another, as if they were a fleet of ships preparing for an ocean voyage or a squadron of planes preparing for a night flight. But for Paco, the rounded hay bales faintly reminded him of scattered marbles. He felt for the ones in his pocket. He touched them—all seven—and they clacked their welcome back. Paco counted the haystacks.

Then, the strangest thing happened. While Paco counted, from the corner of his eye it seemed that where he had just been looking, one of the haystacks *rolled*.

Paco looked back at it: no, it wasn't moving. And yet, the bale, as motionless as a stone, seemed as if it had just moved. Paco felt he had put his eyes back on the hay a moment too late—a moment no longer than the time it had taken to bat an eyelash. The hay seemed to be just finishing its roll, not quite moving, coming to rest like a leaf on a branch returning to stillness after a gentle breeze.

Paco frowned. He riveted a stare on the hay bale like a detective evaluating a suspect from behind one-way glass: no movement. Paco continued counting bales, but after three or four more, he noticed again, at the very edge of his vision—or just outside the edge, really—that another haystack rolled. No sooner had Paco commanded his eyes to return to the renegade hay, than the bale stopped rolling and looked as if it were minding its own business and doing nothing more than counting sheep in its sleep.

Paco furrowed his brow. He carefully turned his face back to the haystack where he had left off counting but kept his eyes fixed on the one he *knew* was faking being asleep: nothing.

The very moment the boy gave up and looked away, the strange movement happened a third time. Paco earnestly wanted to catch the hay rolling, so he determined upon an idea.

"The next time, I won't wait until I see the hay move," he said to himself. "I will look *before* I think it's moving, and then for sure I will see the hay rolling."

Paco proceeded to count again, but this time more slowly, articulating the numbers out loud, so as to deceive the hay bales into thinking that he had no secret plan in mind—no, none at all, other than to blithely count the haystacks in the moonlight.

"Twenty-one, twenty-two…twenty-three…twenty…four…twenty…"

"Five!" A man's stout voice shot through the dark to finish the number.

A floodlight hit Paco so hard he felt as if the very strength of its brightness might knock him off Plod. The horse also froze in the force of what Man calls a "Q-Beam," that dreaded source of a thousand lumens that Bog had railed against in his ode at the stable. But now Bog found himself just as immobilized as his friends, for if there is one weakness that almost every creature has, it is the paralysis that comes with beholding pure light. Patch, on the ground and out of sight behind Plod, dove under the haystack thanks to a small space he found there.

An object fluttered in the glare before Plod, and he found his head passing through a lasso. The light touch of the rope on his neck pushed him out of the stupor of the Q-Beam, but the evasive move he made only tightened the line into a choking wire. Plod saw that the rope, now as straight as a rebar, proceeded from the center of the floodlight and pulled him into it.

"Gotcha!" said the robust voice. "Now what in the Sam Hill do we have here? A boy on the prowl like a bobcat!"

Paco did not know what to do other than grip Plod's mane.

"Boy, what are you doin' out here?" the voice said. "Don't your momma know that you're out? You're in a heap o' trouble, trespassin' on my property."

Paco wanted to reply, but he could not get past the word "momma." It brought up the memory of when he had last seen her. The dark. The noise. The water. Her voice. Her eyes just visible, white with fear and a fierce love, determined to save him.

"Boy, do you speak English?" the Man of the House said. "That's the language on this side of the border, you know."

The Man of the House took hold of Plod's halter.

"Come on, son, you're comin' with me, English or no English. I can't tell if the cat's got your tongue or you're just playin' possum."

The Man of the House, in a manner gentler than Paco expected, led the horse and his boy away. Bog held on, refusing the urge to leap into the dark field behind him. But it would be less than fully accurate to say that Bog met the Man of the House with his "eyes in front" as he had boldly proclaimed to Patch. Bog had closed them, pulled the mane about him like a cloak, and prayed for daylight. Plod and Paco were captured.

* * *

Oracle searched for the singing quail. Low to the ground he crept, more stillness than motion, every hair on his coat alive, every placement of a paw a careful choice. His wide, unblinking eyes never left the spot in the darkness from which the song had come. But when he reached it, he only found empty mesquite, whose sleeping branches spoke nothing to him. On the ground was a single, small feather of brown and gray with downy white at the quill. Oracle looked beyond the branches to the stars above.

"I did not hear them fly away," he said to himself. "How can a flock depart without the beating of its wings?"

He turned to the moon.

"Where did they go?" he asked. And the moon gazed at him with knowing, glowing sympathy.

And as Oracle beheld her shining face, the song of the quail played inside him. He heard it, and he listened.

"'Face the south...turn around...Lonely Tree...' The quail is the one bird the allthorn and the cypress told me still remembers the Lonely Tree. Tonight they sang facing south. They must be singing in the direction of the Lonely Tree! I must turn around. I must go in the grace of the jaguar."

Now in the pace of a cat on the move,
Now in the dark by the light of the moon,
Now in the creek of the water blue-green,
Now in the bush and the tunnel unseen.

Oracle headed south. He passed the dune where he had listened. He passed the cottonwood. He passed the forgotten forge of the branding iron. He crossed over caliche roads and secret trails Man had cut for himself in the clandestine journeys he made between the borders of his realms. Oracle continued through the night, until at dawn he reached the deep lake of Bear Claw Ranch.

"Here is where I gathered bruises, and here is where they fade again," Oracle said. And he fished freely for sleek and eager bass.

East he turned, toward the sun, and traveled with the morning light in his eyes. He crossed brackish ponds and the flatlands of the horned lizard and the cactus. And each moment the scent of the sea grew stronger. He crested a clay bluff, and there he was: brother sea, the Gulf of Mexico, the sibling of the great Lady River. On his marshy waters, the sun played and sent a silent orchestra of colors through the waking clouds.

"Good morning, you who border the realm of the Lonely Tree," Oracle greeted. "I cross land I have not yet seen to find what I seek." And the sea washed his weary paws with the bubbling song of his gentlest waves. Oracle turned south, traveling all day through field after field of morning glories and railroad vines.

When the sun had set, Oracle heard the song of the quail again, coming from a dune whose silhouette was just visible in the dusk. A clump of partridge pea bushes hosted the song, but in the waning light, he could not see the birds. His first impulse was to hasten to the partridge pea to ask the quail to speak an exact map to him, but then he remembered how his attempt to meet the quail in the mesquite had only made the song stop and the birds disappear.

"If the song stops by my coming close," Oracle reasoned, "then I will permit the song to keep singing by my being still." And so, the Lord of the Valley listened. This is what he heard:

We face the west
Where stands the Blessed
Beyond the waters bent and long

We turn to right
When it is night
Remembering the ancient song

We see the tree
The Lonely Tree
Where our grandparents watched in awe

As Kahoo brave
Kahoo the Grave
Recited prayer, gave up the paw.

Oracle took in the song of the unseen quail until every word had found a home in his memory. He turned right and walked west. Even after he had moved out of earshot of the quail, they continued to sing to him from the place where he had hidden the song in his heart. On he went through stands of scrub oaks and sprawling tallows. On the other side, he found a rustless fence topped with ironthorn and a sign so new its smell still stung:

EDEN'S BEND

Paco did not know what to do other than grip Plod's mane.

CHAPTER 15

THE LEAP

PACO felt small in the worn, French Provençal chair the Man of the House had placed him in. He was in the maid's room, just off the kitchen. In an upper corner hung a flat screen TV, Bog's "black pond of Man." There a reality TV show jabbered, the expletives of its contestants censored so often that the dialogue seemed more like Morse code than words. In that night's episode, men and women were on a sailing ship in the Antarctic Sea, attempting to reenact Shackleton's 1916 ordeal between Elephant and South Georgia Islands. The contestants were arguing about something. Paco took a careful look at the boat. The hatch had no door, just a canvas covering.

"That's easy to open," he thought. "Not like the door on my boat."

The man of the house offered Paco a root beer. He took it, but it seemed too cold to him. He put it down.

"Where are my friends?" he asked.

"Oh, so you *do* talk," the Man of the House said. "How should I know where your friends are? Who *are* your friends? It'd be good for me to know. I'll phone them instead of the sheriff."

Paco thought about his three traveling companions, whose language was not that of the Man of the House. He said nothing, and a long silence followed, which the cursing contestants on the TV's storm-tossed ship filled with noise.

"Where you from, anyway?" asked the Man of the House.

"Mérida," Paco said.

"Mary what?" asked the Man of the House. "You must be from south of here. Figures."

Paco looked toward the kitchen. At the window above the sink, he noticed the seal-brown back of Plod, who was swishing his tail. The Man of the House noticed.

"Oh, is *that* one of your friends?" he said. "I tied him up until I can figure out who he belongs to. I reckon he ain't yours."

A woman in cold cream and curlers emerged from a long, picture-cluttered hallway, which, without the lights on, resembled the mouth of a cave. She wore turquoise terry cloth bath slippers, a pink robe, and dollar-store glasses that corrected her vision to the precise distance needed between her pillow and the screen of the nineteen-inch Zenith on her dresser.

"Who's this?" she asked.

"A kid who was snoopin' around."

"Did he take anything?"

"Nope, but he tore up our security camera and that 'lectric eye thing."

"Young man," the woman said in a loud voice, "how comes it that you tear up somebody's stuff? That ain't right."

"I didn't do anything, Tía," Paco replied. "The raccoon did."

The woman tilted her head and looked at Paco above her glasses, eyes unnaturally wide due to the angle of her face.

"Oh, I see…the raccoon did." She did not blink until she rolled her eyes toward her husband's to send a microwaved message: "We've got a live one here, don't we?" The Man of the House grinned.

* * *

Out from under a haystack, a nose in white fur probed the air for danger. It assured the rest of the body that all was clear, and Patch emerged from beneath the bale of hay. His nose told him the direction his friends had gone, and he followed the trail that lingered in the air.

Patch tracked the scent until he heard Bog's song. Patch's ears joined his nose in the search for his friends, and they led the raccoon to the driveway of a manplace. Patch heard the toad singing from a great shadow where the house formed an alley with a two-story garage. A steel-paneled gate, trimmed in white, sealed the side that stood before Patch. A security camera watched the tall barrier.

"I can't climb the gate. If I do, the eye will see me, and the Man will come out," Patch said. "But if I go to the far side of this manplace, I will find the kinds of trees Man likes near his dens."

On the far side of the tall garage, Patch found what he had hoped for. He climbed a palm, jumped to a banana tree, and found a stalk that met a rain gutter. He climbed up the gutter like a bear, crawled across the roof like a cat, and peered down like a fox. Below him stood Plod, tied to the burglar bar of a first-floor window, patiently swishing his tail.

"Plod!" Patch whispered. "It's me!"

Plod's ears turned and pulled his head up with them.

"Well, hello there," said Plod. "Didn't know if you'd make it to our little get-together here."

"Where is the manchild?"

"Inside."

"Do you think we can get him out?"

"Won't know until we try," Plod said. "Now, if you could give me a little help with this rope, I'd be much obliged."

The door from the manplace opened. Out came the Man of the House and his wife.

"So, this is what you found snooping around?" the Terry-Cloth Lady asked.

"Yep. The kid was ridin' on it."

"And you're gonna call the police?"

"I don't know. The kid barely talks. I think he was just wandering around."

"Pulling out wires while he was 'just wandering around'?" said the Terry-Cloth Lady. "I don't think so."

The Man of the House untied Plod while the Terry-Cloth Lady opened the gate. Burt and Mel drove up with a rusted, brown horse trailer attached to the ranch car, a '96 Bronco—the red had faded so badly that, in the blaze of the driveway's bug-clouded arc lamp, it looked pink.

"Opal, did you see that Craigslist post on the missing horse from Eden's Bend?"

"Yeah, it's a match," she said. "This is the horse all right. Says it was a leftover on the property when that rich kid Tripp MacPherson bought it. They want it back anyway so they can get rid of it proper next time there's a meat truck headin' for Mexico. But there ain't nothin' in that post about a missing kid. Somethin' ain't right."

"I know," said the Man of the House. "That's what spooks me. I think the sooner we get these two trespassers down to Bud, the better. If the folks at Eden's Bend wanna pick up their stray horse, they can get it from the sheriff and deal with the problem of this illegal in front of Bud's boys. I don't want nothin' to do with it if there's traffickin' goin' on."

Burt and Mel got out of the Bronco, weapons in hand. The Man of the House ushered Paco into the truck. Then he led the horse into the trailer and tied the halter's rope lead to a U-shaped aluminum bolt at the fore. He clanged the trailer gate shut and slid the rusted bolt to keep it that way. He turned to the ranch hands, who were steadily watching the darkness beyond the reach of the arc lamp.

"You two stay here and keep an eye on the property," the Man of the House said. And he also turned to peer into the night, which hid all things both real and imagined from his sight. "Saddle up the ATVs. I'll call you when I'm on my way back."

The Man of the House remained on watch while the ranch hands stepped into the garage. The Terry-Cloth Lady watched the Man staring hard into the darkness. She tightened her bathrobe and went inside. As she locked the deadbolt behind her, the ranch hands rolled out two bright-red, all-terrain vehicles. The Man of the House got in the driver's seat of the Bronco. He looked at Paco, whose arms rested one on top of the other in his lap; head was turned turned to catch a glance of the trailer from the corner of his eye. The Man of the House started the engine.

Twenty feet above, Patch watched the manmachine growl itself awake. After a flash of the reverse taillights, the truck and trailer began to inch forward, taking Paco, Plod, and Bog away.

Patch realized he had the space of one breath to make a decision. It was much too short a time for such a choice, but as he inhaled, he remembered Oracle. He remembered how clear things had become when the jaguar breathed on him, and in that memory, he knew who he was and what he should do. He did not merely remember the secrets in the rings of his tail. He remembered his name. Patch leaped.

The raccoon hit the aging metal of the trailer. The Bronco's throbbing engine drowned out the sound. Patch, scrambling for something to cling to, flattened his body to dodge the force that warred to shove him off the back of the moving metal. Patch appealed to the rust on the trailer top to help him. Though resentful, it obliged and gave the raccoon all the friction it could offer. The rust slowed Patch's sliding enough to give him time to think as his hind legs dropped off the back and slowed him a millisecond more until he found the bars of the back door. He lunged at the bars as he dropped, locking his arms about them while the manmachine picked up speed. The Man of the House banged truck and trailer along the caliche road of Gaston Ranch en route to the paved county road at the main gate.

Patch climbed into the trailer and dropped to the vibrating floor. Plod turned his head, but only slightly, for the bound rope lead prevented him.

"Nice of you to come along," Plod said, "though I don't know why you'd want to. The Man is taking me back to my owners. It doesn't serve you well to come with me when you have Miracle to round up."

"*You* need to round up Miracle too," Patch said as he climbed to the place where the halter's lead met the U-bolt. "If I get to the lighthouse without you and Bog, what will I say to the Something New I told you about at the stable? He's the one who sent me. He told me to take the boy to the lighthouse, and you and Bog can do just that. Either we all go, or none of us go."

"Hear, hear!" saluted Bog from the tangle inside Plod's hair.

Patch climbed Plod's mane and found that the lead had been tied in a slipknot.

"I've seen this before," Patch said as he squinted at the puzzle of loops. "Yes, at the Rite of the Fourth Ring, the elders showed it to us. Now let me see…they said it comes loose if I pull the…the 'handle' they called it. Hmm, that part looks like a handle…"

Patch pulled once, and two things happened. The lead came loose from the U-bolt, and the trailer slowed down drastically. Patch fell to the trailer floor as his weight shifted without warning.

"What's happening?" he asked.

"Traffic light," said Bog. "The Man has reached the paved place."

The trailer filled with an amber glow that flashed on and off, a four-way caution signal. The air shouted as car after car passed. The Man of the House waited for a gap in the traffic.

"Can you turn around?" Patch asked Plod.

"No, it's too small."

"Then you'll have to back out," Patch said, and he climbed the horse's tail. He jumped upon the door. He jutted his paw outside. He found the latch. He slid it aside. The door swung open from the tilt of the trailer, carrying Patch with it to open air. Plod's rear hooves were on the ground when the Man of the House accelerated. Plod reared and cleared the trailer. It rattled into the intersection. The Man sensed the sudden lift of drag, heard the banging trailer door, turned the truck sharply to return to the gate—and jackknifed his rig beyond motion. Vehicles rushed toward him from both directions.

Paco, in the front seat, now facing the ranch entrance, saw his friends.

A distant car horn grew as loud as a freight train and met the protest of rusty iron. The collision flipped the empty trailer on its side, twisted the back of the Bronco, and shoved it rudely forward.

The Man of the House slapped his hand onto the hazard-lights button and jumped from the car. A driver and his passengers emerged from a yellow lowrider—gaunt orange in the flashing yellow light—wedged into the folded-up metal of the trailer like a fist punched into a beanbag chair. Words flew from angry faces that looked jaundiced under the pulsating traffic signal.

"Man, what were you thinkin'!" shouted the driver. "You can't see headlights?"

"Just hold it right there," the Man of the House said as he threw his hand up on the end of a stiff arm. "No sense gettin' angry. I've got a loose horse and a—"

It occurred to the Man of the House to see if the boy was OK, but when he glanced at the Bronco, he saw an open door and an empty seat. In the dirt at the gate, footprints and paw prints disappeared into horseshoe tracks, and these disappeared at the cattle guard, a series of slippery steel tubes embedded in the ground, meant to keep cows from escaping when the gate was open. Beyond the cattle guard, hoof prints gouged the earth and vanished behind a curtain of switch grass and juniper on his neighbor's property.

Sleeping on the ground was a trampled electric wire, what the animal kingdom calls a "firestring."

* * *

"Here we are," said Oracle as he considered the fence of Eden's Bend. "This is the place of the last resaca, the great loop going north and turning south again, where I said farewell to Patch and Miracle. I watched them go down the old trail to the old stable. And I followed the bend until it no longer led north. But ah! Now I see! The quail sang of 'waters bent and long'! They sing of this, no doubt, for it is west, where I have turned. I must find the resaca."

Hovering just above the fence was the branch of a Mexican olive tree whose branches generously spread above and beyond the wiry boundary line. Beside Oracle grew an oak that leaned from wind and age. He climbed the oak. He leaped upon the olive branch, and he climbed it until he reached the trunk on the other side and shimmied down. And so it was that the oak and the olive trees helped Oracle enter Eden's Bend.

Oracle surveyed the air.

"What strange aromas do I smell?" Oracle wondered. "And strange tracks do I see—animals not of Sian Ka'an but also animals whose tracks I have not found in other places in the Valley. What tribes are these that live here and nowhere else?"

Oracle continued west, wondering what he would do when he found the great, looping resaca again, when, on the other side of a stand of Mexican ash trees, he found a road white with new gravel.

"It is the road I saw before with Patch and Miracle!" he said, and he followed it as it bent west, then south, then west again.

He paused. At the last visible bend south, he saw young anacua trees that seemed faintly familiar to him. But in the distance directly west, Oracle spied a gathering of willows. A great stand of them gave way to other varieties of trees in a line northward. The scent of fresh water reached him. Away to the left, an old windmill worked in vain to fill an unseen, muddy hole.

"It is the long resaca, the end of one of her arms bending south!"

Oracle stood watching and wondering what to do, when suddenly from the midst of the distant willows, he saw the flickering of a strange light. It was not a flashlight, but a dim, yellow eye that blinked. It moved a bit and then hovered in the dark. Beside it a red point of light burned with fixed and threatening certainty, then disappeared. But the yellow eye remained. Oracle felt that it was watching him.

"It is Man!" he said. He returned up the road to the ash trees in haste, but behold, a dim, yellow eye appeared in the shadows of their branches as well, as if calling back in silent response to the strange light beneath the willows.

"Man again!"

Oracle ran southwest, cutting through fields of wild rye and savannah grasses. He reached the young anacuas by the gravel road and dove into a culvert beside them.

Oracle looked up at the anacua saplings. They waved their tender branches in the wind with joy.

"Welcome!" the saplings said. "Welcome, Lord of the Valley!"

"Can you tell me the way to the Lonely Tree?" Oracle panted.

"Yes!" they replied. "Seventy springs our mother has waited to see you!"

CHAPTER 16

TO DO AND TO BE

O RACLE rejoiced at the news of the young anacua trees. "Thank you!" he said. "Where is she? For I have heard the Tale of the Last Jaguar, and I have come to complete it."

And the saplings sang their reply:

Our mother dreamed
About a prayer
That in the air did linger
It never died
But ever cried
Through blooms that were its singer

We know the song
That hovers long
It is the prayer our mother
Has waited years
In drought and tears
For answer from another

She is the tree
The Lonely Tree

We are her seed and children
She is not far
Indeed you are
About to find her hidden

Beyond the vines
Where ivy twines
Behind the leaning stable
There you will see
The Lonely Tree
With grace if you are able.

Oracle rejoiced. "Thank you!" he said.

A faint crunching sound reached Oracle from beyond the bend in the unpaved road, growing ever louder in mechanical steadiness. The jaguar rose and loped straight south. He found a refuge of brushwood just as the manmachine appeared on the road driving slowly, headlights off. It stopped at the anacua trees. All was quiet.

Oracle continued south, with all the stealth of his feline tribe, through the secret tunnels of the undergrowth. He reached the southern edge of the brush where drought had turned the plants into a hedge of brittle twigs. In the foreground were stacks of steel mesh panels and poles, components of fences yet to be built. Stakes with fluttering, orange ribbons marked future work that stretched away to the horizon. And lo! In the distance, Oracle saw the dilapidated stable Patch had entered. Oracle reached the beaten path that led to it. He surveyed the ground with his nose. Yes! Here they were: the tracks of Patch going in and out of the little door within the gate! And here were the tracks of the boy—going in only. But coming out: the tracks of a horse! And the tracks of the horse and the raccoon went *away* on the path together until they entered a sorghum field and disappeared among bent stems.

"Well done, Fair Bandit!" rejoiced Oracle. "You have made friends for Miracle! Well done!"

Twigs snapped, betraying the presence of another. Oracle looked toward the drought-dead bushes, and there he saw the dim green eye of Man. Beside it the red light burned, tiny but fixed. As Oracle looked about for the best way to flee, he saw in the direction of the windmill—north—another distant, strange-colored flash.

"What is this? The lights speak to one another again!"

Oracle darted behind the stable. There he found a tangle of vines and ivies that no one had cared to clear for many a spring.

"The place the saplings spoke of!" Oracle exclaimed. "'Behind the leaning stable'!"

He hunted for an opening, but the vines were so thick that not even with his whiskers and paws could he detect a passage.

"I must push through," he said, and he closed his eyes and penetrated the vines. They gave way, but only to his shape, and not a hairsbreadth more. They slid and snagged and brushed along his sides, not deliberately resisting the cat but not serving him either. There was a moment when Oracle felt himself so enclosed in the bramble that he wondered if he would every get out again. But Oracle felt his nose break free of the tangle, and then his face. He was through it. He opened his eyes.

There she was, the Lonely Tree. She was tall and old with bark of evening gray, filled with furrows from the deep thoughts of a hundred winters and as many springs. Her leaves, even in the night, revealed a green deeper than the myrtle and the fir. The upper surface of the leaves, aged and rough like sandpaper, gave the sound of sorrow as other leaves brushed against it, while the underside, soft as the face of a youth, gave a sigh of joy. She leaned with age but still retained the arms Kahoo had climbed and the memory of that moment. Oracle spoke.

"Greetings, Lonely Tree. Greetings from the jaguar Oracle. Greetings, oh tree, who was there the day the last jaguar died. You live in his story. You remember."

Hail to you
Who heard the jaguar's cries
Hail to you
Who tells the butterflies
Hail to you
Whose branches keep the tale
Hail to you
Who whispers it to quail.

The Lonely Tree responded in quiet exultation.

"Welcome, Lord of the Valley, the one who awakens me from the troubled solitude of seventy springs. Welcome to the place where the Tale of the Last Jaguar is complete and the Tale of the New Jaguar begins. Welcome at last."

"I have heard of your fragrant blossoms," Oracle said. "Their beauty has even reached my ears far to the south in Sian Ka'an of the Yucatán, where I am from. And this is why I have come. To find you, oh Lonely Tree, who bathed my distant kin, Kahoo, in fragrant farewell when Man cut the cord of life from him. Thank you for bathing him. Thank you for taking to heart his prayer, that it would not be forgotten until someone answered it."

And Oracle sang an ode to the Lonely Tree:

You remember everything that happened
You were here, and here you have remained
You have savored sorrow like a banquet
You have waited and have not complained

I have come to answer supplication
I have come to heal the bitter pain
I will pull the thorn of lamentation
I will close the wound and wait for rain.

The Lord of the Valley lifted his head to the night sky. The moon and the stars watched him with wide-eyed anticipation, wreathed in the thick vines who had gathered along with the heavens to keep watch with the Lonely Tree for seventy springs behind the forgotten stable.

"Oh moon and stars, you have waited long," Oracle said. "I still do not understand how a jaguar comes 'from the north and from the sky,' but I do understand that I am a jaguar who can set his paws where Kahoo's tracks have faded, at least until—as Kahoo prayed—'another comes to rule the kingdom.' Perhaps my turning around at the song of the quail fulfilled the word to come 'from the north' when I journeyed to the wasteland of the cottonwood tree. Perhaps. You know, oh moon and stars. You see. Keep watch with me until Kahoo's words untangle from their riddle and become an answer strong and straight."

And Oracle sang an ode to the last jaguar:

I have heard your twilight prayer
I have heard your moaning
Faithful ones have carried it
Through creation groaning

You have left this ruddy earth
You have joined your fathers
I remain to keep the watch
And to kiss the waters.

I will gladly take your place
I will gladly follow.

I will open up my eyes
Fill up what is hollow

Who can come here from the north?
From the sky so endless?
Who has wisdom? Who has worth?
In a realm so friendless?

Here are paws upon the ground
Doing their own choosing
Stars and moon without a sound
Keep the prayer from losing

Any word or any part
I can't plan or reason
Heaven knows the willing heart
Heaven knows the season.

Farewell Kahoo of the Tree
I'll take up your story
Carry it inside of me
Into Eden's glory.

The Lord of the Valley placed his paw on the anacua.

"For seventy springs your name has been the Lonely Tree, but today you are no longer alone. I have heard the prayer of the last jaguar. I have come. Since I am with you, your name is no longer Lonely. It is Lovely. For you have waited in sorrowful hope, and hope fulfilled is a tree of life for you."

The Lovely Tree leaned back and forth, her branches gently brushing one another and the vines that had hidden her for so long, as the wind passed through them and embraced them all.

"Oh, how good of you to have come!" she rejoiced. And the quail came. They descended onto her branches and sang. And there in the depth of the warm August night, the Lovely Tree knew spring, and she bloomed. Her fragrant blossoms bathed the tangled vines, who breathed in the sweetness until every thorn and bitter root fell away, and all became a verdant wreath of joy.

* * *

The travelers heard the sea before they saw it. The junipers of the sleeping ranch beyond Gaston's forbid the view. But Plod made a way through the final row of trees by stepping on a leaning fence post until it became a footbridge through the weeds between the trunks. On the other side, bluestem and primrose gave way to sand. The sea laughed to see them coming from such an unexpected place among the junipers.

"All there's left to do is follow the beach," Patch said. "The lighthouse will be on our right very soon."

The travelers reached it. An ornamental light burned in the glass cupola above, but no one tended it. For no one relied on the lighthouse anymore, except as a sign of forgotten stories known only to those who took the time to read and to listen. Stories of brick and of battles. Stories of storms and of sea catches. And silent boats that never returned. And silent beachcombers who longed for them.

A manicured lawn, thick and green and well watered, surrounded the white tower in a perfect square. Beside this was a place with stone benches and a great, granite slab, slanting like an altar. On it a large brass plate told visitors about the lighthouse.

The travelers walked in a quiet circle around the lawn. It was empty. They inspected the benches. They were bare. They tried the black, iron door at the base of the tower. It was locked.

"Papá!" cried Paco as he looked toward the sea. "Where are you? Are you here or there or in the sky behind the moon? Where are you, Papá?"

The boy looked at the moon.

"Mamá!" he cried. "Are you swimming in the sea where last I saw you? Are you swimming in the moon where the lakes play? Are you in the tower but cannot speak? The iron door is like the one on our boat. Did you bring it here? Did it float? Where are you, Mamá?" And he wept on the back of the horse while the beast of burden hung his great head low and did not graze but breathed on the earth below him a prayer of sorrow.

Bog hopped off the horse and went to Patch, who sat perplexed on the brass plate. He fingered the manletters on it, wondering what they said and whether they gave a sign to where Miracle's parents were. Bog spoke to Patch.

"This is a great tragedy, to be sure," he whispered. "But if we remain here much longer, the dawn will bring Man, and our search for the boy's parents will be a tangle of trouble. We will not be able to do what your friend, the New One, has told you to do."

"Yes," replied Patch, "I know. Let us leave here."

The travelers returned to the beach. They found a slope that led to a low place where partridge pea and bluestem offered shelter out of sight from the lawn of the lighthouse.

Patch stepped on something smooth and solid. He lifted his foot: a marble shone in the moonlight. He stared at it. Paco joined him. He saw the marble too.

"My friend!" cried out Paco. "My friend I left at home! How did you get here?" He peered into its moonlit colors. They spoke to him of the sea.

"Mamá carried you, didn't she?"

The moonlight grew clearer on the surface of the glass, such that Paco saw a tiny disc of the moon reflected on it.

Paco held up the marble to the moonlight with two fingers and a thumb, admiring it like a diamond. The marble told him a story.

The horse whinnied softly. Paco turned.

Beneath his hoof was a battered lifejacket. Paco grabbed for it as if he were drowning. He pressed it to his face. It was damp with Gulf ocean and bilge water.

"I see! I see! Mamá carried my friend from Mérida, and Papá carried Mamá to here!"

Exhausted, he lay down among the railroad vines and made a pillow of the life jacket. He dreamed of a hot meal in Mérida with Mamá and Papá—a dream so vivid that even after he awoke, it seemed to him that the air smelled of *recado rojo*.

* * *

Plod, Bog, and Patch considered what to do.

"We should take Miracle to the Sanctuary of the Sabal Palms," Patch advised.

"What?" Bog said. "A long journey! Many dangers! How shall we get there?"

"I do not know how to get there," Patch replied, "but I do know we can search until we do. And once we get to the Sanctuary of Sabal Palms, we can wait for the New Thing I told you about. He plans to go there too. Perhaps he will even reach the Sanctuary before us and be waiting. Either way, it will be a good thing to be with him. He is very wise. He will know what to do with the boy Miracle."

Plod placed a gentle hoof forward. "I am for it," he said. "No good doing a job halfway. Let's find him a home. We've got a lot of ground before us, but searching for the right path isn't quite the same as being lost. Worry no longer about the sweet drink you borrow for me, Patch. I will feed my legs with the food I find growing along the way. Do not risk your fur anymore. I am content to be a horse and not a hireling."

"If Plod goes, then I go," Bog said. "I have become at home in his mane. I have become at home in this long walk."

And so the travelers departed across a vast and dune-filled savannah in search of the Sanctuary of the Sabal Palms.

* * *

"It is time to find the stewards of the Valley," Oracle said to the Lovely Tree. "I must meet them and offer an unclawed paw. If they accept it, we shall hold a Council of the Cats at the place of their choosing. We shall summon the feline tribes, whoever remains and whoever hides. And they shall remember their names. Then the kingdom of the Valley will be ready for a Court of the Animals at the Sanctuary of Sabal Palms."

"Farewell," said the Lovely Tree. "Farewell on your journey. Go with grace."

"Without that none can go, be they on four legs, two legs, or wings."

Oracle departed through the vine passage he had made. He emerged in a space of shadow and derelict farm tools. Across the space was the leaning stable, asleep and empty, with no memory at all of Bog or Plod or their miraculous visitors. The moon poured its light down upon the stable, though its glow was strictly the moonlight and none whatsoever of shine or reflection. For the rust and the plywood could not comprehend the light.

Oracle's ears tensed as air pressure suddenly shifted in them.

"Someone is near." He listened.

A scrape. A sound. Steps on pebbly ground. A bush complaining. Air straining. Oracle lifted his nose and took in the darkness. Above the stale odors of the stable, he caught it: fresh sweat under a layer of musky cologne.

"Man."

He growled. He ran. Branches of wild olives and palo verde formed an escape route. The ground descended on a manmade levied slope. He passed a sleeping earthmover beside exposed loamy earth. On his right he saw a new manplace, unlit but bright with new wood and shining glass. Beyond this was naked savannah. Oracle bounded across it.

"I shall go south. I shall find the Lady River again and ask her for news of the stewards, Pace the ocelot and Force the bobcat. They must learn that the Lord of the Valley has returned and the season of seventy springs is over!"

But even as he finished this thought, he saw ahead of him a fence taller than any he had ever seen. It was made of the same rustless steel he had noticed stacked together near the gravel road and the stakes with ribbons. It was taller than a deer could leap. It was taller than *he* could leap. He would have to climb it and brave the ironthorn on top. But look! To the right! Rising from the blackbrush the shadows of Man! And with their strange lights another strange sight: the men had goggles that hid their eyes and glowed green. And from their midst in the brushwood, a long, metal rod grew, shining in the moonlight. Above the rod a needle-thin red beam cut through the shadows and followed him. As he passed by, he heard a metallic *click*.

Oracle raced for the barrier. He leaped upon it and climbed. Halfway up, the burning eye found the jaguar's broad shoulder. A dart struck. Oracle kept climbing. But as he reached the ironthorn, his shoulder fell asleep. He fell back onto the ground.

He turned. There they were: men in black with glowing eyes and electric torches that threw the strange, yellow light he had seen flashing from a distance. The red eye found the place on Oracle's body where tawny fur faded to white. Oracle roared, his stocky frame poised to defend. Another dart struck him.

He flinched. He called out the cry of his tribe, the first roar the land had heard since Kahoo the Grave had walked there—a rhythm of sounds that spoke of earth and water and longing. The moon and the stars heard and watched.

The eyeless men emerged from the brush, unafraid.

Oracle faced them, struggling to remain alert. He warned them and crouched to spring, but a curtain of darkness descended first over his vision, then his body, and finally, his consciousness. The jaguar fell.

The men lifted their goggles and turned on the torches strapped to their foreheads: cold, white fire of LED bulbs burned a hole into the night. They stood next to Oracle. One man held a deer rifle aimed at the cat while the other two knelt down and gazed.

There he lay, the jaguar Oracle. His red-gold, spotted body rose and fell, and warm rainforest air wafted up in an invisible steam to the minds of the men breathing it in. Oracle's canine tooth gleamed against his black lip; the slight squint of his closed eyes a snapshot of his last act of will before the darkness had overtaken him.

With a trembling hand, one of the hunters—the youngest—reached out and touched a rosette spot.

"We got him."

"Yep, Tripp will be pleased."

"Pull up the truck. Let's get him out of the Valley before sunrise."

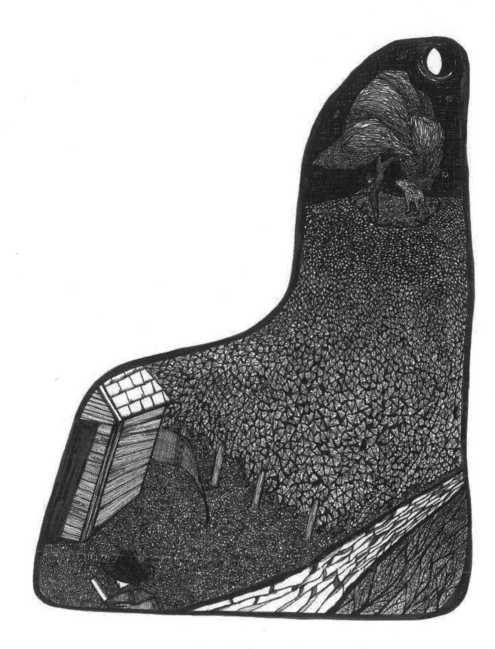

"Oh, how good of you to have come!"

CHAPTER 17

THE MOON AND THE DEW

F ar to the north of Eden's Bend, the truck left its desert track and
sped on an unlit two-lane highway. Tranquilizer rifles filled the
gun rack on the rear window. Night-vision goggles and tools
were piled in an empty backseat. A hunter slept with his head upon
the pile for a pillow, while, in front, his two fellow hunters swigged
energy drinks and talked to stay awake.

"We're makin' good time now that we're on the road."

"Yep. You texted Tripp?"

"Better than that—I sent him a pic. Too bad the jaguar wasn't
awake for it. He looked dead, but I assured Tripp we hit him perfect
with them darts. We put enough M99 in that cat to take out a grizzly."

"What's our ETA to Waco?"

"Noon, I reckon. We're stoppin' in Three Rivers to get the van
with AC. Figure that might take a while since we gotta transfer our
passenger. Tripp will have the zoo fellas ready to receive us at the
service gate. Told us to text him when we're 'bout an hour away so
all the head honchos can be there for a quiet little celebration."

"Great. That'll sure make history. Imagine: a real-life apex
predator extinct for seventy years back in Texas! I'm glad we got him
before the San Antonio Zoo did. They're gonna be jealous, ha!"

"Well, we were just plum lucky. If we hadn't found him on
Tripp's land, we'd have had a hard time takin' him without steppin'
on someone's boots."

"You're right."

"The sheriff was closin' in too. Word is that a cougar spooked Oso's prize bull a couple nights ago, but I'm bettin' this here cat was the culprit. It's good we got him out of Dodge before Bud's boys shot him. Then he'd have shown up stuffed in the lobby of the county courthouse instead of eatin' steak in a zoo, Waco or otherwise."

"But if Waco don't got no papers on the critter, what's Tripp gonna do when the news goes public that he snuck him in like that?"

"I don't think it's gonna. He's given too much to the zoo for them to blow the whistle on their deepest pocket. Half them animals are there because of him. They'll cross their p's and q's in time."

"Don't you mean, 'mind their i's and t's'?"

"Huh? No, I mean what I said; they'll mind their p's and q's in time."

"Oh..."

"And Tripp'll have plenty more critters to give 'em once his exotic ranch at Eden's Bend is built up."

"How long you think that'll be?"

"Not long. There's already a few gazelle and kudu runnin' around down there. We're settin' up better fences for the bigger game and buyin' up some of the land on the east side of Bear Claw. Tripp's lodge is gonna be a beauty: all windows and cedar! But golly, that property hadn't been taken care of for ages. It's like the former owner just completely forgot about his land when he left the Valley. We couldn't salvage more than a few items from the structures. Leveled most of 'em. Kept the stable 'cause of a horse he left behind, but it got loose, and we still haven't found it. I got a phone call from Gaston Ranch I gotta return after we're done with this night run. Might be a lead. Hey, could you hand me another Monster? I'm startin' to drift."

And on they rode.

* * *

Oracle awoke to the droning of a manmachine beneath him. A smooth metal floor, warmed by his body, told him he had been there for some time. It vibrated with news from the road below until his nose itched, and it swayed him back and forth until his stomach became queasy. A strange heaviness pressed upon his brain. Oracle pulled on his memory; the pain in his shoulder and chest reminded him of what had happened.

He lifted his head and surveyed his surroundings. He was in a crate. A narrow, barred window ran along the sides above him. The door to the crate, a few inches from his eyes, featured a bigger window, crisscrossed with steel rods. Outside was the dusty bed of a truck with stake-board sides. Stars peered in faintly between the slats. The air smelled of diesel fuel and desert.

The moon watched the manmachine. She trimmed it with a galvanized glow, and her light flooded the truck bed. Through the spaces between the stake boards, her beams leaned in parallel forms, moving as the vehicle moved. They bypassed the bars of the crate windows and peered into Oracle's container. They found the upturned face of the jaguar.

The moon spoke. Oracle understood. "What are you doing here?" she asked.

"They have taken me, and you and I shall see what we shall see."

"How can I help you?"

"Shine your light."

"Gladly. I shall touch your cheek and lean on your side. I shall form a pool within your eyes. Only, forgive me when I move on."

"It is well," said Oracle. "I know you have a dance to follow that is your own and not mine. Even so, for as long as you can, lend me your light."

"I will talk to the clouds," she said. "I will consult the sun. Do not fear."

And they sang to one another, moon to jaguar and jaguar to moon:

Thank you for drinking the light that I give.

Thank you for giving a light as I live.

Thank you for letting me swim in your eyes.

Thank you for being my friend in the skies.

And they communed this way until the moon was low enough in the sky to look Oracle directly in the face.

"How are my friends?" the jaguar asked.

"All is well," the moon replied. "They have helped one another pass through danger, and now they are friends indeed."

Oracle beheld the moon. Her beauty cast a gentle glow of silver gray that did not hurt to gaze upon yet did not leave the beholder unaffected. The more Oracle beheld her, the more the subtle shapes and lines on the surface of the moon dissolved. No longer did they appear to be the form of anything he had seen before: a rabbit or rooster or any other creature belonging to the tales he had heard. Instead, the shapes became the rippling surface of a mirror—solid yet liquid—very near though unreachably far. He saw Paco in the reflection.

There he was, the boy Miracle, gently rocking on the back of a weary but wise horse. And at Plod's feet, sniffing the air occasionally for caution's sake, was Fair Bandit, the friend of Oracle: Patch the raccoon. And though Oracle could not see Bog, he knew another friend was with them, for a small mound in the mussed hair of the horse's mane revealed his presence.

"It is well," Oracle said.

* * *

On a dirt road winding through a forest of palo verde trees, Paco raised his eyes to the moon. Her glow washed over his face, and, though far away, it made the boy feel as if the moon were very close, right there with him and his friends among the palo verde, the leaves of which faintly bore the argent glory of her presence.

As Paco beheld the moon, her fair light drawing him to look more deeply, it seemed to him that the faint shapes of her surface no longer lay still. They moved as if they were the face of a pond, and unseen great fish were just beneath the veil of the surface. Plod continued in his regular rhythm, but Paco shifted his body so that his face remained perfectly fixed on the shimmering, silver-gray shapes of the moon.

The silent, swirling forms grew sheer as they shimmered, and this is what Paco saw: the face of Oracle. Just how Paco could see this, he could never explain. Later in life, when Paco had a much greater vocabulary, he still could never find words better than "clear" and "clean" to describe the vision. Paco did not take the lunar landscape and intentionally fancy it to be the face of his friend—"That crater makes an eye; that blotch is his nose." It was more fluid than that. Though the surface shapes were indeed the things Paco looked upon, the *face* of Oracle—complete in its parts, composed in its demeanor, and balanced in its proportions—was at once both *on* and *beyond* the variegated hues of silver, white, and gray. Without the moon and her splotchy pockmarks, Paco never would have seen the jaguar. And yet, it was not the composition of shadow and light that contained Paco's friend. These things were pale, but Oracle was rich and alive in them—or perhaps through them. Paco could not tell.

"There he is," said Paco, "the one who said to me, 'Tell me your story.' I told him, and he listened and took in my tears. It's good to see him. I knew I'd see him again. Thank you, moon. You've been watching us. You've been watching all along, haven't you?"

Paco and Oracle beheld one another. A love flowed—a sentiment and a knowing—and it magnified the glow. It enlarged the moon, and the moon, though larger now, withdrew to the background of her light so that the two friends might bask in it more fully without her added company. She did not mind that, though the boy and his jaguar loved one another through her, they were not at that moment aware of her.

"For to reflect their love is to receive it too," she said, "and that is enough for me."

Oracle breathed. The breath lingered about him and turned to joy. The joy filled his face, and his face filled the moon. And the moon reflected the blessing upon Paco and his friends. Plod, Bog, and Patch, moving humbly with eyes toward the road, breathed it in. Their pace did not change, but the air they breathed did. And now the palo verde on either side of them seemed to be singing in a thorn-free world.

Paco laughed for joy. He was not afraid! The darkness, though still dark, was no longer sinister, and the light, though coming from afar, seemed to blanket him as a mantle. And the loneliness became loveliness, the desert delicious, and the hunger good humor. The light had gone into him. Paco beamed it back to the moon and the moon to his friend, the Lord of the Valley.

Oracle, full of that joy, closed his eyes in contentment. He dreamed of romping between the rippling, orange ribbons on the wooden stakes he had seen in the fresh-turned earth of Eden's Bend.

* * *

Paco awakened four of his marbles to see the moon. One by one, he placed them in the cup of his hand, careful to keep his arms poised separately from his hips, which wobbled according to the movements of Plod beneath him. *Click. Clack.* The marbles emerged in the moonlight and took on her glow. *Click. Clack.* They whispered to one another in marvel, "A waning moon shining brighter than a full one!" The marbles traded moonlight with one another, sharing their beams in hushed and tender tones, knowing that light like this was rare and should be celebrated with reverence.

Paco watched the light of the moon dance between the marbles. He laughed. He had never seen them so amazed! This was no common game in sun and dust. This was the game of another playing through them—a game that did not hurt, a game that did not trample, but a game that brought out colors from inside each marble that even the marbles themselves had not known about. It was as if the marbles were finally in the element they had been designed for, and all the dusty childhood games had been rehearsal.

The light played. Sparks like fireflies shot here and there, beams deflected by hidden angles within each marble that cast the light back into the air. Some of these sparks fell on the palo verde trees about Paco. Some fell on the boy's body, some on his face (though of course he could not see these), and some on the neck of the great, weary horse that carried him: Plod, gentle and faithful, unaware of the marble sparks that christened him.

* * *

Above, in the glow-rich air between earth and moon, the owl Salt took his turn keeping watch after relieving the falcon. He beheld the friends traveling through the sleeping realms below. In silence he made a great arc beneath the moon. This is what he saw upon the earth: Lady River glistened on the horizon. Directly below him the friends followed a trail through the choked labyrinth of the palo verde. And in the vast space between the travelers and the Lady River lay an electrified grid of beam and fence and road—the realms of Man.

"If it were not for the prayer of Kahoo long ago, I would doubt the travelers could ever get through the realms that stand between them and the guarded corridor beside the Lady River. But prayers, like dew, settle where they will and have no regard for fence or border. Perhaps the prayers have already descended upon the Council of the Cats and the Sanctuary of Sabal Palms. Perhaps they already wait at river's end where jaguars used to kiss the Lady River. If so, then there must be a way for the Lord of the Valley and his friends. Though my eyes do not see it, the prayers do. Yes, the prayers do."

Salt soared higher until the horizon of the sea shone faintly in the east. He took in the vista of the Rio Grande Valley from his aerial moon perch: Man's lights burned in one pinpoint spot after another, countless false stars glowing blue white or white pink or amber in a great band between the rural lands and the river. But, in contrast to the incandescent efforts of Man, the light of the moon shone far more generously. It covered everything, manplace and green, open and tangled, wet and dry, salt and fresh. It invited the owl to go deeper into the light.

Salt soared higher and higher, golden eyes closed. He breathed deeply. Then he caught it: the scent of the dew. It was descending to earth! He had flown into its coming! Salt opened his eyes and hooted.

"I welcome *you!* I welcome *you!*" called the owl. He ascended for another moment and then turned in a barrel-roll maneuver and dove swiftly. He adjusted his flight to a slow spiral to escort the falling dew.

"I welcome *you!* I welcome *you!*" Salt called again. "You who come from deep within the sky and cover everything on earth! Rough and smooth, thorn and leaf, skin and feather, iron and wood! You who do not wait for me or Man or anything! You who drench all with the essence of the moonlit sky! I say you are a good sign! A good sign!"

The owl danced amid the airborne dew and sang this song:

The moonlight and dewfall
With prayer from the tree tall
Cannot be rescinded
For they have descended.

They're drenching the earth realm
The thickets and sea whelm
Each wide field and shadow

And manplace so narrow

Refreshing our hoping
As path we are groping
With eyesight that's thickened
And all our fears quickened.

We search for the way bright
That brings us to daylight
Through trappings and terror
And mistakes and error

In thorns and frustration
A groaning creation
That's bent and that's broken
Yet still holds the token:

An echo of Eden
When friendship was even
'Tween barefooted children
And snakes in vermillion

'Tween jaguar and raccoon
And gator 'neath full moon
When no one was lonely
And love there was only.

In silence of dewfall
And moonglow, this night owl
Has seen what is hidden:
The road back to Eden!

"Though my eyes do not see it, the prayers do."

EPILOGUE

From Book Two of *The Jaguar Oracle*
The Search for the Shadow Cat

B UT for mice gathering morsels, none yet knew that the place of the jaguar and the place of the tiger were empty at Cameron Park Zoo. None yet knew that they had reached the waterless moat, the last line between the zoo and the outside world. None yet knew that the Men who had clocked out of the day shift left the service gate open, expecting a late UPS truck at any moment. The truck had never come, and the Men of the night shift had never known it was expected.

Oracle peered above the edge of the moat. There, beyond an empty road and an open gate, wound the Brazos River. Crash the tiger joined him.

"If there were ever a moment to make a run for it, it's *now*," Crash said.

"But the edge of the moat is alive with fire," said Oracle. "The crickets have warned us. If you are still, you can hear the flames humming in the wires."

"I'll go first, then," said the tiger. "I still have my circus days in me; jumping through a ring of fire was as easy as licking my paws back in the day. It can't be much different with the invisible fire. It will just sting for a moment, if at all."

Crash went over the top before Oracle could stop him. Just as Crash pushed his way between the stinging fence lines, motion-sensitive flood lamps threw an unnatural blast of light upon him. The tiger urged his body forward. The firestring burned, but not for a moment as he had thought; it traveled into him like an angry liquid seeking the center of his bones. He shouted. He twisted involuntarily in pain, tangling in the lines. He fell backward, and his heavy frame pulled the firestring with him. As he hit the bottom of the moat, the wires ripped away from their posts. The firestring died.

The spider monkeys shrieked in alarm, swinging in frenzy through their rope trapeze. The flamingos cried out through a flutter of flapping wings. The buffalo moaned her long call of warning, and her calf, beside her, cried out as if forlorn. Every animal in the zoo awakened.

Oracle had two choices before him: remain with his blundering friend, who was suffering at the bottom of the moat, or escape before Man arrived.

Oracle looked at the Brazos, its flat, wide waters moving silently away. Beyond sight it passed southeastward through a city park and college campus to the woods and their hiding places. Oracle looked at the tiger, wincing as the last of the invisible fire dissipated in his body and new pains from the fall took over.

The sound of an electric manmachine whined at high speed up the path.

"Go!" cried Crash. "Go, both for you and for me! Greet the cats in council you told me about! Greet them with my courage and my roar!"

"What courage is it for me to leave you behind?" asked Oracle. "To leave you and live would be a half-lived life."

"But the *Council*!" shouted the tiger. "The Valley *calls*!"

The manmachine rushed into view, and Men leaped out even before it had fully halted. They came running, arming their weapons as they came with a *click-clack-click*, black rods that spat both needles of sleep and bullets of death. One never knew which would come, and at that moment, the Men themselves did not know either.

Oracle knew what to do.

* * *

Patch reached the top of the tree first. The final branches rocked him back and forth. Cradled where he could no longer climb, he viewed the Sanctuary of Sabal Palms. Five hundred acres of forest stretched away beneath him, trees of palm, of cypress, and of the ebony that now held him high. In the distance, the Lady River glinted back a gracious greeting to the relentless sun. Beyond her was another land, the manrealm Mexico, where roads and ranches lay very still and half real behind the horizon's chalky haze. Patch followed the edge of the sanctuary with his eyes as it retreated back toward him in obedience to the great curve of the Lady River. And as he followed the tree line, his eyes fell upon a strange sight: another lighthouse! Or was it? He looked closer. It looked like a tower, but there was no tiny manplace on top of it and no beacon of light; just a point like the end of a spear.

Paco reached the top. He saw the tower too.

"A lighthouse!" he shouted, but at once he realized that it had no light on top or a glass house to hold it. Still, he wondered.

"Maybe Mamá and Papá went there because they did not find me," he said. He hastily clambered down. Patch followed headfirst, turning his hind feet fully around so that the descent was as graceful and rapid as the climb. At the bottom, Patch announced the find to Bog and Plod.

"But there is only one lighthouse in the Valley," Bog insisted.

"I know, but it's tall like the other one," Patch replied. "Maybe Man is building a new lighthouse."

"Perhaps," said Plod. "No way to know except by going there ourselves."

"And if we go," Patch exclaimed, "maybe we'll find Miracle's parents! Then we can deliver the boy to them and return to the sanctuary to wait for the New Thing to come! Yes, yes, that's it! That's what we should do! What a kind tree this has been! Now let's see what Miracle—"

Before Patch could finish his words, the sound of breaking underbrush reached the travelers from the shadows of a thicket of sabal palms, a sound accompanied by the obedient moan of an electric manmachine.

Paco climbed on Plod with the help of a stump. Bog hopped into Plod's mane. He sent a message to the toads of the forest for directions on which way to go, but no toad croaked back.

"Run or hide?" Patch asked. "Or fight? What do you say, Bog?"

"I say the silence of my tribe tells me that something comes to us that is as bad as the pit bulls we escaped—or worse."

"Miracle is sitting very still on my back," Plod said. "Let us follow his lead and do the same."

They waited. The sound grew, and if it did not bring Patch any hope, at least it pushed away the memory of his fright with the pit bulls.

"Here they come," Bog said, but this time—which for Bog was the first time—he met the danger with eyes wide open.

It was not what the travelers had expected. A Man appeared in a small camo-patterned machine. His hair was white and somewhat long, gracefully swept back with oil, and his mustache, which was just as white as his hair, was so large that it was hard to tell if the Man was happy, or angry, or neither. But his eyes had a spark in them, a flame of resolution. The Man stopped his machine.

"*Buenas tardes, muchacho,*" he said. "Another traveler hiding in the Sanctuary of Sabal Palms, I see! Who are you?"

"I am Paco, and these are my friends," the boy said.

"Ah, friends," the Man said, looking them over with a pondering frown. "Good to have in these times, if true friends can still be found. But if not…Tell me, son, what are you doing here?"

"I went to the lighthouse to find Mamá and Papá, but they were not there. Then this tree made me tall, and I saw another tall place. It is far away. It looks like a lighthouse, but it has no light on top. I know they are waiting for me. Maybe Mamá and Papá are waiting for me there even though there is no light."

"Maybe," the stranger replied. "I know the place. It is behind a barrier three fences deep. And you are right: there is no light on top. It is not a lighthouse, my boy. It is a tower very different from that—a tower that lifts off the ground with fire and goes far up into the sky, farther than any cloud or bird can go. And if Papá Eli could do it, he would climb into that flying tower and go up there, too, and never come down."

"'Who is Papá Eli?'"

"That is me, son. They call me Papá because I have lived much longer than people normally do in my profession. And that is why I am here. I am trying to *retire*, you see, but that is a word too big for you just now. I live near the tall place, but I come here whenever I have—well, special guests at my house."

"Can you take me to the flying tower?"

"I can take you to my ranch when my guests leave. It is near the flying tower."

"My friends are coming with me," Paco said.

Papá Eli looked at the horse and the raccoon sitting beside him. The two animals remained watchful, silent, and still. Bog, in the horse's mane, was not yet visible to the Man.

"The horse can come," said Papá Eli. "But the raccoon, no. He cannot."

"But the raccoon must come," insisted Paco. "He knows how to rescue marbles. He knows their secrets. He knows the story of the one I rescued from the water when Mamá and Papá went away."

"Your Mamá and Papá disappeared in the water?"

"Yes, that is the last place I saw them. But they came to shore, I know. I saw the grassy spot at the lighthouse where they were. I am looking for them."

Papá Eli shook himself as if awakening from an unintended nap. "Wait! You came here from the *sea*? How long ago?"

"I do not know. I have not counted. All I know is that the moon helps me. She is smaller now than what she was at first. And she told me the good cat was going to be OK."

Papá Eli craned his neck forward and stared at the boy. Astonishment fell over his face.

"You...you...Paco, who was the uncle who captained your boat? Tell me."

"The uncle? Tío Sergio. That was his name. I saw his gold tooth shining in the dark, and that is how I found him after the boat went away. He lost his sunglasses. I know because when I swam close I saw the whites of his eyes. He was very afraid. I was too."

Papá Eli's jaw dropped. He breathed in a deep, sharp breath and pondered heavy thoughts before placing a pleasant smile upon his face.

"Paco, my son, come with me to *El Pequeño Jardín*. That is my ranch. I will help you."

"Help me find my parents?"

"Help you find out," Papá Eli replied, and he looked away from the lad.

"You will take me to the tower that is not a lighthouse?"

"I will take you to the owner of the tower," Papá Eli replied. "He is my neighbor. He lives at Eden's Bend."

Papá Eli led Plod to the back of his vehicle and tied the rope lead to a bar there. Paco looked back at Patch.

"I will not go without my friend," the boy said. He slid off the horse and dropped to the gound, his bare feet meeting a mat of dead leaves with a thump. He went to the raccoon and stood tall in his smallness beside his friend and the ebony tree.

Papá Eli was silent. He climbed into the driver's seat and lit a Cuban cigar. For a moment, the old man's face was hidden within a bluish cloud of tobacco smoke, the aroma of which was so strong that the boy's eyes stung and watered when it reached him. But when the smoke cleared, there was no water in Papá Eli's eyes. He removed the cigar from his mouth and looked toward the thicket of the palms.

"Well, son, it seems to me you have to make a choice. Either stay here with your friend in this unfriendly forest where strangers appear from behind the trees, or come with me to find your parents." He began to drive away, slowly. Plod followed, constrained by the rope.

Bog turned and called to the raccoon. "Wait here with Miracle, Patch!" he said. "Wait for the New Thing you told us is coming! Yes, be faithful to the end! Farewell, my friend! Farewell! Give the New Thing our greetings! And remember my last words: *to the end*!"

"I...but you...I shall run after you!"

"Neigh," called Plod from his tethered head. "The Man takes us. It is the way things are with our kind. Stay with Miracle. Wait for the New Thing. Keep well." And he swished his tail in farewell.

Paco gave Patch a desperate look. Then the boy stared with pleading eyes at his departing friends and the Man who knew the way to the flying tower. The manmachine grew smaller as Papá Eli guided it into the shadows. Plod, following on the lead behind, passed through a small cloud of bluish smoke.

Paco knew what to do.

Made in the USA
Charleston, SC
06 April 2016